BETWEEN HERE AND FOREVER

Also by Elizabeth Scott

Bloom
Perfect You
Living Dead Girl
Something, Maybe
The Unwritten Rule

BETWEEN HERE AND FOREVER

ELIZABETH SCOTT

Simon Pulse
New York London Toronto Sydney

SIMON PULSE
An imprint of Simon & Schuster Children's Publishing Division
1230 Avenue of the Americas, New York, NY 10020
First Simon Pulse hardcover edition May 2011
Copyright © 2011 by Elizabeth Spencer
All rights reserved, including the right
of reproduction in whole or in part in any form.
SIMON PULSE and colophon are registered trademarks
of Simon & Schuster, Inc.
For information about special discounts for bulk purchases,
please contact Simon & Schuster Special Sales at 1-866-506-1949
or business@simonandschuster.com.
The Simon & Schuster Speakers Bureau can bring authors
to your live event. For more information or to book an event contact
the Simon & Schuster Speakers Bureau at 1-866-248-3049
or visit our website at www.simonspeakers.com.
Designed by Tom Daly
The text of this book was set in Berkeley Oldstyle.
Manufactured in the United States of America
2 4 6 8 10 9 7 5 3 1
Library of Congress Cataloging-in-Publication Data
Scott, Elizabeth, 1972–
Between here and forever / by Elizabeth Scott. —
1st Simon Pulse hardcover ed.
p. cm.
Summary: When her older, "perfect" sister Tess has a car accident
that puts her in a coma, seventeen-year-old Abby, who has always
felt unseen in Tess's shadow, plans to bring her back with the help
of Eli, a gorgeous boy she has met at the hospital, but her plans
go awry when she learns some secrets about both Tess and Eli,
enabling her to make some decisions about her own life.
ISBN 978-1-4169-9484-8
[1. Coming of age—Fiction. 2. Sisters—Fiction. 3. Secrets—Fiction.
4. Coma—Fiction. 5. Self-perception—Fiction.] I. Title.
PZ7.S4195Be 2011
[Fic]—dc22
2010051366
ISBN 978-1-4169-9486-2 (eBook)

Many thanks to Jennifer Klonsky and everyone at Simon Pulse for all they do, for their continual faith in me, and for making this book possible.

As always, thanks go to Jess, Diana, Clara, Robin, and everyone else who read drafts and held my hand and supported me, with a special shout-out to Jess, who always finds time to tell me that yes, I can do this.

I also want to thank the following readers for being such amazing and supportive people: Morgan Mavetz, Brittani Zarate, Jenny Davies, Katy Williams, Jessica Launius, Lucile Ogie-Kristianson, Denise Jimenez, Kalie Spurgas, Amber White, Andrea Burdette, Christina Rose Groff, Jhenne' Martinez, Kat Werner, Stacey Mac, Sarah Wethern, Marina Ornelas, and Jess Faulkingham.

one

I lean forward and look at Tess.

She's still.

Silent.

The machines that keep Tess alive beep at me. I've been here so often that sometimes I think they're her way of replying. But today that's not enough. Sunday is a day of prayer after all, isn't it? So here's mine:

Today I want Tess to wake up.

Today she has to wake up.

I lean in, so close I can see the tiny blue lines on her eyelids marking where her blood still pumps, still flows. Shows that her heart still beats.

"If you don't do something, Tess, I—I'll sing for you."

Nothing.

"I mean it," I say.

Still nothing. Tess's eyes stay closed, and her body lies limp, punctured with needles and surrounded by machines. I used to visit Tess with Mom and Dad, used to wait with them for the doctor, but the news never changed and I got so I couldn't bear to see my parents' faces, washed out and exhausted and sad.

Like a princess in a fairy tale, Tess is asleep. Deeply asleep.

I guess "coma" doesn't sound as good when you're trying to sell stories where everything ends up okay.

Sleeping means you'll wake up.

Coma . . . well, coma doesn't. And Tess has been in this bed, in this room, in this hospital, for six weeks. She was in a car accident on New Year's Day, driving home the morning after a party. She'd waited to come home because she didn't want to risk getting into an accident with a drunk driver.

Instead, her car hit a patch of ice and slammed into a tree.

Tess was always so good at being safe. At doing the right thing, at making people happy. And now she's here. She turned twenty in this room, four days after the call that sent us all rushing here. My parents got her balloons. They floated around for a while and then wilted, fell.

Tess never saw them.

I turned seventeen in this room too. It was two weeks and two days after the accident. I was still visiting Tess with my parents. They got me cupcakes from the vending machine and sang when I opened them.

BETWEEN HERE AND FOREVER

Tess didn't say a word. Didn't even open her eyes. I chewed and swallowed and chewed and swallowed even though the cupcakes tasted like rubber, and my parents watched Tess's face, waiting. Hoping.

That's when I realized I had to start coming by myself.

When I realized I had to bring Tess back.

"Wake up, Tess," I say, loud enough for my breath to stir her hair, and pick up the glass unicorn Beth brought the first time she visited. She said she knew Tess would like it, that it was all about impossibilities. I thought that sounded a bit beyond Tess, who dealt in the here and now and in being adored, but when Beth put the thing in Tess's limp hands, I swear she almost blinked.

Now Tess doesn't do anything, and I put the unicorn down.

I miss the little ledge where it sits though, and it hits the floor. It doesn't break, but a crack appears, running from one end of the unicorn to the other.

A nurse comes in and frowns at me.

"Accident," I say, and she says, "Love is what your sister needs, not attitude," like it wasn't an accident, like she knows me, like she and all the other nurses who have only ever seen Tess in this not-life, this twilight state, know her.

They don't, they can't. But I do. Tess believes in happily ever after, in dreams come true, and I've decided that's how I'm going to reach her.

Now I just have to figure out how to do it.

I leave the hospital and ride my bike down to the ferry.

Once I'm on board, I stand by the side of the boat. Most

3

people stand up front; the wind in their hair, the river all around them, and Ferrisville up ahead looking almost quaint and not like a big pile of nothing.

I look at the water. It's dark, muddy brown, and slaps hard against the ferry. I can see my shadow in it, all chopped up, bits and pieces scattered among the churning waves. I turn away, because I already know I'm broken, that there's nothing in me worth seeing. I already know there's nothing worth believing. It's just how I am.

two

I run into Claire when the ferry's drifted into the dock at Ferrisville and people are heading to their cars.

"Hey you," she says through the three inches her window will roll down, jamming her fingers through the opening into a sort of wave. "Wanna ride home?"

I gesture at my bike. "You got room for this?" Claire's car is about the size of a cracker, and littered with Cole's stuff. There's barely room in it for Claire.

She rolls her eyes at me. "Yes, but go ahead and leave it at the dock. You know nobody's going to steal it."

"Are you saying my bike is shit?"

"Yeah," she says, and I grin at her because it is a pretty shitty bike. It was nice when Tess got it—back when she was ten—but now it looks like a beat-up old bicycle that someone's younger sister got stuck with.

Which, of course, it is.

I ask Daryl, who normally stands around scratching himself but today is standing around coiling rope, if I can leave my bike on the dock.

"Sorry, no," he says, and then, "How's Tess?" in the voice everyone uses on me now, the oh-it's-such-a-shame voice. The oh-we-all-miss-Tess-so-much voice.

"Not dead yet," I say, my voice cracking, and drop my bike by his feet before I stomp over to Claire's car.

I hate how I am when people talk to me about Tess. I hate how everyone sounds. I hate how she's already been reduced to the past when she isn't.

She's still here.

"You okay?" Claire says when I get in.

"Not really," I say, pushing a box filled with what I hope are new diapers onto the floor. "I just . . . the way people talk about Tess. Like she's gone."

"I don't think it's totally like that," Claire says. "I just think they miss her."

"Do you miss her?"

Claire looks at her hands on the steering wheel. "Me and Tess stopped talking a long time ago."

"You mean she stopped talking to you because you dropped out of high school to have Cole."

Claire sighs. "It wasn't—it wasn't like that, Abby."

But it was pretty much exactly like that, and we both know it.

"How is Cole?" I ask, finding an open pack of gum on the floor. I wave it at her. "Is this stuff still good?"

Claire takes the package and sniffs it. "Smells like fake fruit. Go for it. And Cole's fine. I have the only two-year-old who's afraid of toilets, but he's fine."

"Maybe he just doesn't like your bathroom," I tell her, popping a piece of gum in my mouth. The flavor bursts sweet and fruity across my tongue, but only lasts about two chews. "I know I'm afraid to go in there. It's like being inside a cross-stitch classroom, with all the reminders to put the seat down and wash my hands."

"So funny. Like your mother's collection of towels no one but 'guests' can use is better."

I shrug and shove another stick of gum in my mouth. "I heard one of the nurses talking about her kid today. He's four and sometimes takes off his pants and poops on the rug. So I figure you're doing okay with Cole."

"No! Who is it?"

"Kathleen."

We grin at each other. Kathleen is Claire's supervisor, and is always making Claire run and fetch things for her, like Claire's her slave and not a nurse's aide.

"That almost makes up for how she acted today," Claire says. "She spent five minutes yelling at me for having a stain on my pants when she knew the reason I had the stain was because she made me wash Mrs. Green, who always pees the second you start to bathe her."

We pull onto Claire's street, which is also my street. Cole is out in the front yard, running around after Claire's dad's hunting dogs in that weird way little kids have, where for a second it seems like they're going so fast they're going to fall right over their own feet.

"Momma!" Cole yells at Claire when we get out of the car. He can say about ten words now, although Claire swears he's talking when I think he's babbling.

"Hi, baby," Claire says. "Wanna say hi to Abby?"

"No!" Cole says, which I don't take personally because of the ten words I know for sure that Cole knows, his favorite is "no."

"Hey," I say, and pat the top of his grubby little head. "Claire, thanks for the ride."

"Sure," she says. "Tell your parents I said hi, okay?"

I nod, but I won't. Telling my parents anyone said anything would mean actually talking to them, and that's something that doesn't happen much these days.

After all, what is there to say? We all know what's going on. We've all waited and waited for Tess to wake up.

We are all still waiting.

three

"How was the ferry?" Mom calls out from the kitchen
as I come in. I stop, shrug at her, and then walk upstairs to my
bedroom.

My parents have to take the ferry home from the hospital too,
so they know what it's like. There's no other way to get from Milford
to Ferrisville, and the ferry is what it is, a slow boat on a river.

There was talk, once, of building a bridge, but nothing
ever came of it. My guess is that if Milford wanted a bridge
across the river, it'd be built in a heartbeat. But why would they
want to connect to Ferrisville? We're a small, poor town near
nothing but acres of government-owned land that's supposedly
a national park or reserve. Not that we get any visitors. Who
wants to see something called "The Great Dismal Forest"?

Even more importantly, who wants to live near it?

Well, my parents, for one. They think it's nice we live near a river, that on the weekend we can walk down to the water and trip along the sand-studded rocks (that's "the beach") and look at people grilling or riding around in tiny boats, their motors roaring as they pass each other going back and forth, back and forth.

But of course my parents like it. They didn't grow up here. They grew up in a nice suburban neighborhood, with shopping malls and neighbors who aren't all related to each other in some way. Or so they say. My mother's parents are both dead, and my dad doesn't talk to his parents at all, and they only ever mention where they're from once in a while.

Tess used to love to look at pictures of them from back when they first started dating, and even before, from when they were in high school together. She asked all sorts of questions that neither of my parents ever really answered. It's like they didn't exist until they met each other and moved here.

Tess used to say our parents had secrets, and lots of them, but that was back when she was stressing out over going to college, and had also stopped talking to her best friend just because she got pregnant. And that made her into someone I had no desire to listen to.

I figure there won't be any follow-up questions to the nonquestion I got about the ferry, but just when I'm feeling almost relaxed for the first time all day, Mom comes up and knocks on my door.

"Abby, what are you doing?"

"Homework."

I'm not. I don't need to, because Ferrisville High is a joke, but I need to be alone right now. Try to figure out what to do about Tess.

"I wanted to tell you that your uncles sent Tess flowers again," she says. "Did you see them?"

"I must have missed them. Sorry." I'd seen them, and read the cards. *Get Well Soon* on each of them, and nothing more. My mom's brothers, Harold and Gerald, seem nice enough, but they don't come to visit often.

Mom's not that much older than they are, but it's like—well, the couple of times they've been here, they treat Mom like she's way older than they are. They treat her like she's their mother, with a weird sort of respect and anger. I don't know what they have to be mad about. They don't live here.

"I'm going to go and make something to eat for your father and me," Mom says. "Maybe heat up the leftover pancakes from this morning. Do you want to join us?"

I want to, but I don't. If I do, I will see Tess's chair. I will think about it.

I will know we are all thinking about it.

"I'd better finish my homework," I say.

"All right then, good night," she says, with a little sigh, and I listen to her footsteps fade away.

four

After school the next day, I grab my bike from the ferry dock (amazing how no one took it, right?) and head to the hospital. I weave through the ground floor, past the waiting room full of people doing just what the room wants them to, down the hall past the gift shop (run by cheery old Milford ladies who chat about their prize-winning dogs or flowers while they sell gum for the outrageous price of two bucks a pack), and around to the elevators.

Everything about Milford Hospital is depressing.

Well, not everything. I like the cafeteria. It looks out over the river, and Ferrisville is far enough away that you can't really see it. You just get an impression of houses on carefully laid out streets, a factory nestled at one end, and a rocky strip of beach dotted with the weathered ferry station.

Plus the cafeteria is the one place in the hospital that doesn't smell bad. Everywhere else smells like chemicals, like the kind of clean that can strip away your skin if you get too close. And underneath that chemical smell there's always another one, fainter but never ever gone.

Underneath, you can smell unwashed flesh and fear and how off everything is. How everyone who's in here, all the patients lying in all their beds, aren't here because they want to be. They're here because they have to be. Or because this is the last place they'll ever see.

The elevator comes and I step inside, prepare to see Tess.

After I'm buzzed in to her unit, I walk to her room. She looks the same; thin, pale, somehow gone but yet still here. Her hair's been washed, though, and it shines, golden against the white of her pillow. A nurse is fixing one of her IVs, and sighs when she sees me.

Tess was—is—always good at getting people to like her.

I suck at it.

"I'm going to change her sheets," the nurse says, and I nod, sit down to wait even though the nurse sighs again, and then Claire walks by like I've somehow summoned her. I start to wave, but she isn't looking at me. She's looking at the unit entrance, and I realize everyone else is too, that all the nurses are turned toward it like something's going to happen. Weird.

Then the buzzer sounds and a guy comes in.

"Tess," I say, leaning over and whispering in her ear. "You're missing your big chance. Everyone's staring just because some guy's come in here, and you know what that means. He must be cute."

Nothing.

"I'm not kidding," I say. "One guy, and all the nurses are looking at him. That means very cute. Just like when you walk into a room."

Then, weirdly, the guy is actually coming toward the room, toward Tess, the nurse who was babbling at me about sheets before hurrying over to him.

"Thank you so much for doing this," she says, all giddy-voiced. "I can't tell you how nice it is of you to help out, and—"

And then she stops talking because she walks right into the door.

I shouldn't laugh, but I do because it's impossible not to—she walked into a door, after all—and she glares at me as she ushers the guy in. I get an impression of dark hair and eyes, but not much more because the nurse is fluttering all around him. And also because I just don't care.

"Now, I thought you could help me lift the patient up," the nurse says to him. "Then I'll—oh, I didn't get the sheets, hold on. Claire—Claire! Oh good, there you are. Would you grab some sheets, please?"

Claire rolls her eyes at me, fast, and then says, "Of course," and heads off.

"It'll be just a moment," the nurse says to the guy, still all fluttery-voiced, and when I look at her, she's blushing.

She should be. She's my mom's age, at least, and the guy is

about mine, I think, which makes what I'm sure she's thinking a felony.

As for the guy, he's pretty disappointing now that I'm finally looking at him. I mean, he's staring at the floor like a lump. He's probably uncomfortable being here, where everything is so silent, and everyone's in the kind of sleep you never ever want to fall into, but still.

Then he looks up and . . .

He looks up, and my brain actually stops working for a moment, because the guy is *gorgeous*. Not gorgeous in the oh-hey-hot-guy way, but actually truly gorgeous.

Beautiful, even. His skin is caramel colored, a warm glowing golden brown, and his hair is so black that even the hideous fluorescent lights do nothing to it, don't make it look greenish or stringy. He's got the kind of cheekbones I've only seen on guys in magazines. Ditto for his nose and chin and forehead, and his dark eyes framed by lashes that Tess would murder someone for.

He is, in short, human perfection. Even if he has gone back to staring at the floor and has his arms folded across his chest, fingers tapping against his skin like he's bored. I lean over and nudge Tess.

"Come on, Tess, open your eyes. This guy is so pretty, I swear he's better-looking than you."

The guy clears his throat at that, and I look at him again.

"What? Oh, right, I called you pretty. Sorry. But you are. I mean . . ." I trail off.

He actually looks at me then, and I feel my face heat, turn back to Tess.

"Okay, here we are," Claire says, coming back and handing the nurse the sheets.

"Thank you," the nurse says. "You can stay and take the soiled sheets away. Abby, can you step out for a minute, please?"

I nod, leave Tess's room, and wander out of the unit to the waiting area. Today there's a middle-aged woman sitting in there, head in her hands. She's wearing sneakers, and both of them are untied. I can tell she's either going to cry or start yelling at any second, so I go sit in the stairwell.

I wait. I'm good at it, I've learned a lot about it the past few months, but when I go back to Tess's room, the nurse, Claire, and the guy are still there, the nurse and Claire talking quietly.

When I walk in, the guy clears his throat again and speaks for the first time, saying, "Um, can I go?"

"Oh, something something something," the nurse says to him but I don't hear it because Tess's eyes twitch. They don't open, but there's definitely movement there, under her closed eyelids.

She's coming back.

"Wait, please," I tell the nurse, who does, and turn to the guy. "Say something."

"Abby," Claire hisses, and the guy says, "What?" Even his voice is gorgeous, low and soft.

I look at Tess. Yes, there was definitely a sort of twitch there.

"Did you see that?" I say to the nurse. "When he talks, Tess can hear him!"

five

The nurse doesn't agree with me. She says I'm overwrought, and then me and Clement take a little ride in the elevator. The nurse is pissed that it's him who comes and gets me, and not someone from security, but Clement points out that at least I'm leaving.

The thing about Clement is that he's about seventy years old and barely comes up to my shoulder. He sometimes gives bored little kids a "top secret" tour of the hospital, but mostly he just walks around talking to people.

He's not a real security guard, obviously. But he did give about ten million dollars to the hospital three years ago. For that kind of money, if you want to spend your days walking around the hospital greeting people, fine.

"Are you all right?" he says, and Clement is one of those people who means what he says. I like that about him, so I tell him the truth because I know he'll listen.

"Tess's eyes moved."

"Really? That's wonderful! What did the doctor say?"

I shrug. "Nothing. The nurse won't call him. She said she didn't see anything. She made me leave."

"Do you think that maybe . . . sometimes we see things we want to."

I know about that. I fooled myself into it once, and won't make that mistake again."Hey, I like you, but not that much, so don't think I did all this just to see you," I say, and Clement laughs his wheezy laugh and then pulls out one of the seemingly endless supply of cough drops he's always got on him.

"You shouldn't be so worried all the time," he says. "You'll give yourself gas."

I laugh then too, and he grins at me as we walk outside.

"Go on home," he says. "And take care of yourself."

"Me?" I say. "I don't—I'm fine."

Before he can reply, I get on my bike and head to the ferry.

When I get home, I fry up an egg, and then wedge it between some bread and eat it while I watch television. Mom and Dad get home when I'm flipping through the channels trying to decide if I want to watch the gritty crime drama about detectives who track down missing people, or the other gritty crime drama about detectives who track down missing people.

Mom turns off the television. "You want to tell me about what happened today?"

"Tess moved. Her eyes were closed, but I saw them moving, like she might blink. Or was going to blink."

"Abby . . ." Mom says, and sits down on the sofa. "You can't . . ." She looks down at her hands. My mother's nails are always neatly polished. This week they are a pale pink. "You don't know how much your father and I want Tess to wake up, and saying things like that only—"

"Hurts," Dad finishes, coming in and sitting down next to Mom.

"But I did see her eyes move." This is a good thing, and I don't see why my parents don't believe me and why they are sitting on the sofa looking miserable.

"Remember the first week?" Dad says. "You and me and Mom were there, and you swore she moved her hand when Beth was talking to her?"

"Her little finger," I say. "And it happened."

"Beth didn't see it. And Beth is her roommate and friend, honey."

"She was looking at Tess."

"Exactly."

"No, I mean she was looking at her face."

Dad rubs a hand over his forehead and then leans back into the sofa, closing his eyes. "Abby, we don't want you to think that your sister—" He breaks off, clearing his throat. "Don't be angry at Tess."

"I'm not," I say, but he gives me this look, this I-see-through-you look, and I go upstairs and slam my bedroom door.

I know what I saw today. Tess heard something in that guy's

19

voice, something that grabbed her, and now I know exactly what I need to do.

I can't reach her, but maybe someone else can.

I get up, open my door as quietly as possible, and slip down the hall into Tess's room. It hasn't been touched since the accident, and her bags from school are still on the floor, and photos of her and her college friends are sprinkled all over her desk.

I slide my hands over them, see Tess smiling in the sunshine. She has my dad's bright smile, all warmth, and I wonder about the guy she was smiling at. Did she like him? Or did she like the guy with the black shirt who shows up in the next photo, eyes on Tess and full of longing as she reads something he's holding in one hand?

Or what about the guy two photos later, the one who is grinning at her as she examines a tattoo on his arm, watching her fingers on his skin? Or is it the guy holding the camera in all the photos?

Whoever he is, he hasn't come to see her—none of them has—and Beth, as nice as she is, is just her roommate and can't and won't make up for that.

But that guy today could. I can almost see her sitting up and smiling at him now.

I wonder if she can see it too, and think that maybe, just maybe, she can.

six

I head over to see Claire when I get to the hospital
after school the next day. She's standing in the tiny alcove the
hospital has set aside for smokers, hidden off to the far side of
the building. Milford is a no-smoking town, and self-righteously
proud of it, but Ferrisville isn't, and since Milford people can
afford to go to better hospitals—and do—this is where people
from Ferrisville come. And a lot of them, like Claire, smoke.

I fan the air around me and her, and she makes a face at me.

"I thought you were quitting," I say.

"I'm working on it."

"How?" I squint, pretending I can't see her through the haze
of smoke.

She sighs and stubs out the cigarette. "Fine, Mother. Hey, what did you think of that guy yesterday?"

"He can make people walk into doors."

She laughs. "That was the best, wasn't it? You should see Eli when he's working in the gift shop, though. People stop and just stare at him like this . . ." She makes a zombie face.

"You one of them?"

"No, I'm off guys forever after everything with Rick," she says. "Trying to get him to pay child support—ugh."

"Guys suck," I say, and she shakes her head at me and says, "Yeah. You're lucky you don't have to deal with all that crap. Tess always . . ." She trails off, like she's said something she shouldn't.

Like she's said something I don't know.

Like I don't know that Tess is easy for anyone and everyone to love and I'm—I'm not.

"Hey, I'm glad I don't have to deal with all the stuff Tess did. All those guys calling and telling her that they loved her, or sending her stuff, or wanting to take her out, and me? Well, I don't have that problem at all."

Claire bites her lip. "You know what I meant, Abby. You're very—you have—"

"I have a sister I have to go see," I say, stopping her before she has to try and finish her sentence. "And the sooner she wakes up, the sooner she can go back to breaking hearts. See you later."

Look, I know I'm not pretty. As Tess once told me, not so much to be cruel, but just because she always wanted to know about our family and its history, I have my mom's mother's eyes, a muddy brown-green with weird blue flecks in them, and dark blond hair that likes to defy my brush and nature and just stick up wherever it wants to. Also, I'm built like a twelve-year-old girl. (That part no one had to tell me. It's just obvious.)

And it would be fine if I was still twelve, but barely filling out an A cup at seventeen is pathetic. As is the fact that I can buy—and wear—boys' pants because I'm barely five foot two. And also have no hips to speak of.

But now I know the guy I saw yesterday is Eli, and that he can be found in the gift shop. He must be fairly new to the hospital—I know everyone who works here—and I can work with that. I know what I saw yesterday.

I know what—who—Tess needs in order to wake up.

seven

I tell Tess his name as soon as I see her. She doesn't respond, but that's okay. I bet she needs to hear his voice again. When she does, she'll do what she did yesterday. She has to.

If Tess doesn't wake up, then she isn't—then she won't *be* here. Not truly here, you know? And she's always been the bright star my family revolves around. She's been the person who people in Ferrisville talk about with reverence in their voices. Tess is pretty, young, kind—all the things people want each other to be. All the things people so often aren't.

The only problem is, I don't know how to get the guy up here. I think about it as I tell Tess about my day, mostly lingering on the candy bar I bought before last period because

Tess is a sucker for candy. She even ended up living with Beth because of it.

When I went to visit them last fall, she told me she knew she had to swap roommates and move in with Beth the very first day she came to campus.

"I walk into my room," she said, "and there's this girl sitting on the floor eating a Nibby Bar. You know, the one with the cocoa nibs in it?"

I'd nodded and made a face because Tess's love for bitter chocolate, up to and including chocolate with pieces of twiglike chocolate in it, made no sense to me.

"And I think, wow, this is going to be amazing, because I love Nibby Bars too," Tess had said. "But it turned out Beth lives across the hall, and just stopped by to say hi. I knew things would work out, though. And they did!" She'd turned and grinned at Beth, who shook her head at Tess, but still smiled.

"How about some candy?" I ask Tess now. "A nice bar of chocolate, maybe? I'll get you one, I swear. You just have to open your eyes."

Tess doesn't move.

"Fine," I say, and my voice comes out more angry than I mean it to. I swallow hard and look at the floor.

"Someone wanted a copy of, um, *Sassy You*?" a voice says out in the nursing area.

The voice. It's that guy. Eli. I hear someone else murmur something, but I don't listen.

I don't listen because behind Tess's closed eyes, I see something move. I see her body hearing something. I see it responding.

25

I know what I have to do, and so I go out and say, "It's mine. I mean, I want the magazine."

The guy—Eli—looks at me. If I thought he was really looking at me, and not seeing someone who wanted a copy of the world's stupidest magazine (and if I looked like someone he'd want to see), I swear my knees would melt. (That's right, melt. Screw going weak. Eli is beyond that mortal power.)

"Um, excuse me, but I asked for that magazine," one of the nurses says. "Mrs. Johnson loves it."

Mrs. Johnson is in worse shape than Tess. She can't even breathe on her own, and no one ever comes to visit her. I guess all her family is dead, or something. She just lies there in her room, all alone, day after day, air pumped in and out of her lungs, keeping her breath flowing, her heart beating. The nurses don't pay much attention to her, and the first week Tess was here, I had nightmares about Mrs. Johnson every night.

I started sneaking into her room once in a while and saying hello to her, and the nightmares stopped. I still do it, and although I've never spoken to her, I'm sure Mrs. Johnson wouldn't want a copy of *Sassy You*, with its stupid articles about how to get guys to want you "all the time!" and profiles of celebrities whose greatest achievements are tossing their hair around, smiling, and swearing that their latest trip to rehab "changed their lives."

"So, who gets it?" Eli says, looking at the nurse and then at me. "I gotta get back down to the gift shop. Nobody else is there today."

I point at the nurse and go back to Tess.

"Sorry," I whisper. "I'll—" What? I have no idea how to approach him. I don't approach anyone.

But this is for Tess. For Tess to wake up.

"I'm going now, but I—I'm going to get Eli for you, okay?" I say. "Don't go anywhere."

I pretend her mouth curves up into a smile. I pretend she can hear me. I take the copy of *Sassy You* the nurse swore Mrs. Johnson wanted from where it lies unopened on the stack of magazines the nurses "read" to Mrs. Johnson by standing there and reading the magazines themselves, and shove it in the trash.

"Sorry you had to see that thing," I tell her. "And, hey, I'm going to get Tess to wake up. She has to, you know. Otherwise . . ." I trail off.

Otherwise this is Tess's future. A long, slow decline. A lifetime without life.

A lifetime of me tied here, because if Tess doesn't get better, my parents will give up everything to keep her alive and end up with nothing. I will have to stay and help them, be the rock they can lean on. I will sink into Ferrisville, and I will decline too. I will have a lifetime without a life, and I don't want that.

I know it's selfish. I know a better person, a better daughter, wouldn't think like that. Tess wouldn't think like that.

But I'm not Tess. And the last thing I want is a life in which I do nothing but prove that over and over and over again.

eight

Eli is in the gift shop. I figure he'll be talking to a bunch of girls or admiring his reflection or whatever it is gorgeous people do when they are at work. Tess got a job at a grocery store in Milford the summer before she went to college, but really all she did was spend day after day talking to guys who'd trail around Organic Gourmet after her.

Eli isn't talking to anyone, and he isn't looking at himself either. He's sorting through a bunch of magazines, tapping his fingers against each one and making faces at the headlines. He even scowls gorgeously.

I should probably be nervous about talking to him, but a lifetime of watching guys stumble over themselves to say "Hi" to Tess has made me realize how stupid that is. Acting like you're not good enough to talk to someone usually means they decide you aren't good enough to talk to them. Also, Eli isn't for me, he's for Tess. I'm just making sure they meet.

"I'm sure she'll be better soon," I tell him, pointing at the blond stick on the cover of the magazine he's looking at. "They say the sixth time in rehab's the charm."

"What?" he says, and then looks at me. "Oh. You're the girl who—"

"Has the beautiful sister," I say, just because I know how his sentence will end. It's how it always ends. "Can I get a copy of that?"

"You want a copy of this?"

I don't. I'd sooner poke a stick in my eye than read inspirational tales about how some girl has made a fortune selling T-shirts, never mind that one of her parents is always a designer or hip New York store owner, or look at pictures of raccoon-eyed models posing in clothes no one I know can wear. Or afford.

But what I say is, "Yeah."

He gets up and hands me one, all fluid motion and dark honey-colored skin. I am acutely aware of my shortness, lack of curves, and general blahness.

"Are you sure you want it?" he says. "I saw you make a face when I brought it up for Mrs. Johnson, and you don't look like the kind of person who"—he glances at the cover—"cares about the new and best sunless tanners."

Of course not. I look like me, and the way he so easily dismisses me stings a little, but I square my shoulders, dig some money out of my bag, and slap it on the counter.

While he's making change, I look at the candy. Someone's gone through and—I swear, I think it's been organized by bar size and wrapper color. Bizarre.

"Here you go," he says, handing me my change. "Enjoy your magazine."

I roll my eyes before I remember I'm supposed to want the thing and he grins at me, perfect-shaped mouth showing perfect white teeth, and if I were weaker I'd memorize that smile because I am surely never going to see anything like it again.

"Your eyes—do you wear contacts?" he says.

I freeze, my whole body going numb.

"No," I say. If he says I have pretty eyes, I will—I don't know. I just know I won't cry. Jack said my eyes were pretty once, and I was stupid enough to believe him.

But this guy doesn't say that. He just says, "Do you want anything else?" so polite, so perfect, and I admit that for a second, one stupid second, I want to jump over the counter and lick his neck and touch his shoulders and his hair and pretend I could make a guy like him go weak in the knees.

"Yes," I say, squashing that second, that stupid twinge of want, down. "I want you to wake up my sister."

nine

Eli stares at me as if I've just said, "Hi, I'm crazy."

"But your sister, she's—"

"She's in a coma," I say. "But her eyes moved when you talked. She can hear you. So if you, you know, visit her, she'll wake up. And when she does, you'll love her. Everyone does."

"So you want me to . . . what?"

"I just need—I want you to talk to her," I say. "When her eyes moved, it was—" I take a deep breath. "It's the most she's done in ages."

"Are you going to be there?"

"What?"

"If I talk to her, are you going to be there?"

Oh, I get it.

"No," I say, and point at the case where bouquets of gently wilting plants are kept. "I'll order her some flowers or something, and when you bring them up I'll go to the lounge while you do whatever it is you do when you meet someone."

"I can't," he says. "I'm only supposed to go into a patient's room if there's a nurse or family member present."

"Okay, so I'll be in there, then." He's confusing me. "I won't—I won't talk to you, if that's what you're worried about. I know I'm not . . . like I said, I'm here for my sister."

He leans into the counter, leans in closer to me. It takes everything I have to not step back. He's so—he's so gorgeous. He's—

He's for Tess. I'm doing this for her. I force myself to keep looking at him.

"You're really serious, aren't you?" he finally says. "You really think I can wake your sister up."

I nod.

He laughs.

He actually laughs, eyes crinkling up, hair tumbling in perfect casual disarray over his forehead and down over his ears, and I force myself to smile back, to act like I am unmoved by him, like him laughing at me means nothing. I picture myself as the tiny animal I am, all anger and hard-earned knowledge, claws and fangs and an immovable heart.

I picture Tess awake, and my parents happy.

"I know Clement put you up to this," he says when he's done laughing. "Tell him I got the message and I swear, I'll stop giving away gum."

"Wait, hold up. You're giving away gum?" I say, and hold out one hand like I'm waiting for a pack.

Something else I've learned is that it's best to take the moments where you want the ground to swallow you whole—moments like now—and just get through them. Act like you don't care that you've put yourself out there and gotten pushed away. Or, in this case, laughed at.

"I was," he says. "But I'm not now. Tell Clement I know the gift shop is supposed to benefit whoever it's supposed to benefit, and—"

"Ferrisville," I say, the little animal that is me now claws-ready. "You're working to raise money for people from Ferrisville who can't afford to be treated here."

"I forgot—"

"I bet you did. Let me guess, you got in trouble at Saint Andrew's and got assigned here as some sort of punishment?"

"I forgot the name of the town, that's all," he says. "How did you know I go to Saint Andrew's?"

I laugh, brittle and sharp. "We don't have guys like you in Ferrisville."

"You sound happy about that."

"Don't sound so surprised. You just laughed at me when I asked you to help my sister, remember?"

"I—you're serious?"

"Yes," I say, exasperation creeping into my voice. What's with this guy?

"I'm sorry," he says. "I—look, I really thought Clement sent you here, and I don't—I don't see how I can help your sister.

Seriously. I didn't see her doing anything when I was in her room, and I'm really not the kind of guy girls—"

"But she did do something," I tell him. "And we both know you're the kind of guy girls want. If you—if you say you'll help me—help *her*—I'll talk to Clement and get you out of here. He likes me and he can make stuff happen around here. I'll tell him you're helping me with a project for school."

"Clement doesn't like anyone."

"Wrong. He just doesn't like anyone from Milford," I say. "Which is probably why he spends all his time here even though he's a bazillionaire."

Eli blinks. "Wait a minute. Are you—are you Abby?"

Wow, talk about a gamble that paid off. "Yeah."

"You . . . Clement said you were—"

"He can't see very well," I tell Eli. "When you're old, I think everyone who isn't is cute or something."

"He didn't say you were cute."

Okay, ouch. "Ugly, then. Whatever. The point is, I'll talk to him, and you won't have to work here anymore."

"He didn't say you were ugly either."

"It doesn't matter," I say, but it does, and I just want to get out of here. "I'll talk to Clement, and then you just have to talk to my sister."

"Okay, but I don't think she'll wake up because of me."

"You don't know Tess. She loves gorgeous guys, and you're the most gorgeous guy I've ever seen. You'll wake her up, and when she does, you'll thank me."

"Is she like you?" he says. "I mean, is she—does she just say stuff like you do?"

"No, she's not—Tess's perfect. She's beautiful and smart and everyone loves her. You will too. You won't be able to help yourself. I'll talk to Clement now, and we'll start tomorrow, okay? I would say we should start now, but Clement loves to talk and I have to catch the ferry home before my parents—" I break off. No need to go into that with him. "Anyway, tomorrow, okay?"

"Okay," he says. "Abby." I nod at him, and walk out of the gift shop.

If he says Tess's name like he just said mine, Tess will be awake about ten seconds after he starts talking.

Even Jack saying my name never made me feel so—

Stop it.

I promised myself all that was gone, forgotten, and it's going to stay that way. I made myself strong, I taught myself to know who—and what—I am.

I go find Clement. He's drinking coffee in the cafeteria and looking out at the river, and he grins the second I mention Eli's name.

"Told that boy to look out for you," he says. "I said, 'Eli, there's a firecracker.'"

Well, Eli was right. Clement didn't call me ugly. He just called me an object people blow up on holidays. I'd been wondering a bit about how they knew each other, but now I so don't care. And besides, Clement knows everyone.

"The thing is, I need him to help me with something," I say.

35

"And we both know you know everyone and everything and can do stuff. So can Eli help me?"

"What do you want him to do?" Clement says. "I know how you young girls are about love, Abby, but if you want to go out with him, you should—"

"Oh no," I say. "I don't—this isn't about me. It's for Tess. She moved her eyes, remember? And she did it when Eli was talking. So I know that if he talks to her, he can wake her up."

Clement takes a sip of coffee. "Just like that?"

"I know it'll work. I know my sister. She likes cute guys and Eli—well, he's—you've seen him. If his voice can get her to move, just imagine what she'll do once she opens her eyes."

"He is a good-looking boy," Clement says. "Takes after his grandmother's side of the family, but he looks like his mother too. She's a tiny little thing. Came over here from Japan and—"

I cut him off. "So can he do it?"

"You know what your problem is?" Clement says. "You're impatient."

"You said I was worried before."

"So you're both," Clement says, and takes another sip of coffee.

"Well?" I say, when he doesn't say anything.

"See?" he says.

"Fine, you're right," I say, grinning at him. "So can Eli do it or what?"

"He can help you," Clement says. "And you can help him."

"Well, I think Tess will take care of that," I say. "When she wakes up, I mean."

Clement starts to say something, and then pats my hand. "You shouldn't be—you should like yourself more, Abby."

I swallow. "I like myself as much as I should," I finally say. "And thanks for agreeing to this."

"Don't worry about it," he says. "I was going to have to move Eli out of the gift shop anyway. He keeps giving away gum. And it takes him forever to count out the magazines."

"Sort out."

"I know what I said," he tells me. "I meant count. So I said count."

"All right," I say, holding up my hands in mock surrender, and when he pulls out another of his cough drops, I wave at him and head off.

"You're welcome," he calls out after me, and I walk out of the hospital feeling lighter than I have in months.

This will work. I know it will. I'm going to give Tess what she wants. I'm going to watch her wake up. I'm going to see my family knit itself back together, return to the way things used to be.

I'm going to watch Tess wake up, and then I'll finally be able to get away from her. From seeing her so trapped and helpless now.

From living in her shadow.

ten

I see Claire's car up ahead of me as I'm waiting for the ferry, but don't bother even trying to ride up to her. People take waiting for the ferry very seriously around here, and I don't feel like getting yelled at for "cutting in line," never mind that together, me and my bike make up about a quarter of a car. The ferry still counts us as one vehicle.

And makes me pay for it too.

So I wait, and after I'm ushered on board and everyone has parked and the ferry is finally chugging away from the dock, I go find Claire.

She's standing up near the front of the boat, pushing her hair back off her face with one hand. Claire isn't pretty, but she stands out. She has short hair, barely over her ears, and it's bright red, almost orange. She used to wear it super short, practically a buzz cut. I was ten and Tess was thirteen when Claire first got it cut that way, and Tess thought it was the most amazing thing ever. She had a photo of the two of them down at the beach, the top of Claire's head as sunburned as her nose, stuck in the frame of her dresser mirror for ages.

I wonder what she did with it when she decided she wasn't speaking to Claire anymore. I never asked her. When Tess was eighteen and I was fifteen, I never spoke to her unless I had to.

"Hey," I tell Claire, and plant myself next to her at the rail. The ferry pushes into a wave, and spray mists my face.

"Hey," Claire says. "Heard you went to the gift shop today. I didn't know you were interested in tapping that ass, Abby."

"Tap that ass? What year is it?"

"Rick used to say it," she says, a tiny smile appearing but fading fast, as soon as she's said Rick's name. "Well, he said it about me. 'I tapped that ass!' Do you know he actually called me last night and said he didn't see how Cole could possibly need money since he's 'you know, a little kid, and what do they need?'"

"Sorry," I tell her. "So I guess you told him you wanted to get back together, right?"

"Oh yeah," she says, grinning at me. "You know what the best part was? After I hung up on him, he actually called back and asked again because he thought he got cut off. I don't know what I was thinking back in high school."

"No offense, but what were you thinking?"

"I wasn't," she says. "He wanted to have sex, and I thought it seemed so much easier than being in love . . ." She trails off.

39

"Wait, you were in love with someone? Who?"

She blinks at me, and then looks out at the water.

"Someone who didn't love me back," she finally says. "Not enough, anyway."

"Are they still in town? Never mind, of course they are. Who is it? Did Tess know? Is that why she got so mad when you—?"

"Nice try," Claire says. "But I haven't forgotten you were in the gift shop talking to the guy who's so good-looking someone who came into the hospital actually stopped and took his picture."

"Did not!"

"Did," she says. "One of the nurses saw the whole thing."

"That's just sad."

"He is awfully—I was going to say cute, but he's not cute. He's beautiful. Like, really and truly beautiful. Don't you think?"

"I think he's going to wake Tess up."

"What?"

I tell Claire my plan.

"So because you think that you saw Tess's eyes move—?"

"It sounds stupid when you say it like that," I say. "She . . . look, you were in the room. He talked, and something happened to her."

"Because of Eli?"

"Yes, duh," I say. "You've seen him. You even said he was beautiful just now. And you know how Tess is. She's always wanted to be swept off her feet by the perfect guy. Beth even got her a book of 'classic romantic fairy tales' for Christmas." I swallow. "Or at least that's what Tess said. She didn't . . . she didn't ever show us her gifts. She left them at school and now—"

"How is Beth?" Claire says. "I haven't seen her at the hospital much lately."

"She came a lot at first," I say. "But now she's . . . I don't know. Busy with school, I guess."

"They lived together for two years."

"Yeah, but that's how it is in college. Tess says that when you find someone decent to room with, you don't mess with that."

Claire stares down at the river. "You know, Abby, maybe you don't—maybe you don't know Tess like you think you do."

"Oh, come on," I tell her. "Tess wants to be happy."

"No, she wants everyone to think she's perfect."

"I don't think Tess ever worried about that. Why would she ever have needed to? I mean, she's—"

"Yeah," Claire says. "She's Tess. But still, she could never bring herself to do anything she thought someone, somewhere, might possibly think was wrong."

"You know, Mom used to say Tess wanted things to be perfect," I say. "Do you think that's why she acted the way she did when you got pregnant? Not that I think you getting pregnant was bad or anything, but Tess—"

"I know," Claire says, her voice bitter. "Believe me, I know what Tess thought."

"I'm sorry."

"Yeah, well, I know you did too. You never told her about Jack after all, did you?"

I shake my head and force myself to laugh. It comes out rough, broken-sounding. "No, I didn't. She wouldn't—she wouldn't have understood. I mean, look at how she treated you.

And she liked you. Me and Tess just aren't—we're nothing alike."

"I think . . . I think that you two aren't as different as you think. I mean, look at this plan of yours. You're expecting a happy ending, aren't you?"

"Because I know Tess does," I say. "Because she believes in them. I don't."

"Abby," Claire says, but I shake my head again, as if I can shake off the pity in her voice.

"Don't. Just . . . don't. I know Tess was mean to you and she—I didn't always like her, but she's my sister. I'm supposed to want her to—"

"Supposed?"

"That's not what I meant."

"It's what you said."

"I have to go," I say, and head back to my bike. I stare out at the water, at the Ferrisville dock growing closer and closer.

I don't want Claire feeling sorry for me. I don't want her saying that she knows I used to believe in love and all that crap. I don't want to be reminded that I used to think it was possible for a guy around here, around Tess, to look at me and not see her.

I don't want to think that once I was stupid enough to believe I could be with someone who wanted my sister and make them want me.

eleven

My parents get home earlier than usual and catch me in the kitchen poking pieces of toast into the jelly jar and then eating them.

"You're supposed to put jelly on bread, not put the bread in the jar. And you did eat something else besides that, right?" Mom says, and sits down across from me, giving me her Mom stare. She's really good at it.

"Why are you home early? Is Tess—?"

"She's fine. Your father and I—we decided to come home after we talked to the doctor."

I look around for Dad, but he's come in and gone straight into the living room. Something's definitely happened. "What did the doctor say?"

Mom gets up. "I'm going to make a sandwich. Do you want one?"

"Mom," I say, and she looks over her shoulder at me from the counter and gives me a small, sad half smile.

"It's nothing you need to worry about. We just . . . the insurance isn't going to cover as much as we thought and—well, Tess's been in the hospital for long enough that we're being asked to consider other options."

"Other options? Like what?" I know for a fact that Mom and Dad have read everything they could get their hands on about comas. I also know that they've gone to see a bunch of other doctors, and always come back from those meetings grim-faced.

Mom doesn't answer.

"Mom?" I say again, and Dad comes in from the living room, his mouth curved up in this weirdly familiar smile that, for some reason, sends a shiver racing through me, a flash bolt of panic-fear under my skin.

"I bet you have homework," he says.

"Yeah," I tell him, getting up and turning away so I can't see his face and that smile. "I do."

It's silent, so silent, as I walk up to my room and shut the door, but as I creep out of it and back toward the stairs—I shut my door before I went through it because I knew what was coming—I hear my parents start to talk.

"I hate the idea of Tess going to a home," Dad says. "She's not—there's still a chance. She could still wake up. And I don't want her to think—"

44

"She knows you love her," Mom says. "She knows you won't give up on her. We all know that."

"Katie—" Dad says, and Mom cuts him off, says, "Dave, I just—I'm not you, all right?"

Silence falls again, and then I hear Mom sigh, hear her cross the room.

"I wish—" she says, love and sadness in her voice, and Dad says, "Me too," his voice smothered-sounding, like he's speaking from somewhere far away, or holding something back.

Like he's trying not to cry.

I creep down the stairs a little more, and when I crane my head toward the kitchen I see them holding each other, Dad resting his head against Mom's, mouth pressed to her hair.

The smile he was wearing before is gone, wiped clean, and I realize where I've seen it before.

Tess. Her senior year, and especially before graduation, before she left for college, that was how Tess usually smiled. I just—I never realized it was strained. That it wasn't real at all.

My skin prickles even though it isn't cold, and I'm chilled to the bone.

I move silently back up the stairs, head into my room, and close the door behind me.

twelve

Until I was fifteen, I wanted to be Tess. I wanted her straight, shiny hair. I wanted her ability to always look perfect. I wanted her smile to be mine, I wanted people to see me and have their eyes light up.

I wanted all of those things, and never got any of them.

Tess was kind about it, though. It was her way. She would loan me her clothes, and not tell me to go away when I saw her with her friends. And when guys came to see her—and they always came to see her—she'd introduce me to them.

People in Ferrisville see Tess, even think "Tess," and they think "perfect." And she was perfect.

At least, she was in public.

At home though, sometimes, Tess would—well, she had a

streak of darkness in her. Sounds normal actually, I think, but the thing is, she never showed it outside the house, never took it anywhere that people could see. Not ever.

It wasn't anything big at first. She'd get upset over something and just retreat, fall silent and go into her room, act like she'd vanished even though she hadn't. And then, if someone called or came by, she'd . . . I don't even know how to explain it right. It's like she'd smooth something over herself, push it away, maybe, and she'd be Tess again. The Tess everyone knew, the one who was always so happy, who always showed a smiling face to the world.

But that was for the world. For me . . . well, I remember this one time, when I was twelve and she was fifteen, I went into her room without knocking, hoping she'd let me sit with her and Claire, and she just stared at me like she'd never seen me before.

"Hey," I said, and then she'd smiled, a too-bright and too-sharp curve of her mouth, like she'd forgotten how to smile and couldn't even fake it, and got up, came over to me, and said, "Get out."

She didn't yell. She spoke in this weird, flat voice, almost like speaking hurt her, and when I said, "But—" and Claire said, "Tess, relax, okay?" Tess swung around and looked at Claire. Just looked at her, didn't say a word, and Claire looked away from me, looked at the floor.

I took a step back, and Tess shut the door again, still looking at Claire and never once at me. It was like she'd forgotten I was even there.

That night, at dinner, I asked Tess something—what she was

going to wear to school the next day, maybe, or about her hair, things I knew Tess loved talking about—and she ignored me.

"I think Abby asked you a question," Dad said, and gave Tess a playful nudge with the bowl of salad he was holding.

"I can't do this anymore," Tess said, and again, she didn't shout. She didn't even sound angry. She just sounded . . . gone. She got up and went to her room and wouldn't come out for two days. She didn't go to school, didn't take calls other than to tell people she wasn't feeling well but that she was so glad they called. She was "asleep" if anyone came by. She didn't eat, and I don't actually think she even slept at all. She just did . . . she just did nothing.

Mom stayed home from work the second day, and when I got home from school Tess was out of her room and smiling again. When I asked her if she was okay, she looked at me like I'd asked her a question she didn't understand and then said, "Mom says you have her mother's eyes."

"Oh," I said, hurt because Mom never talked about her parents with me, not ever. I knew they were both dead, but that was it. I hadn't even known my eyes looked like my grandmother's.

"Yeah," Tess said. "Did you know she killed herself?"

"What?"

"She did," Tess said. "So maybe you're haunted." She leaned in toward me. "Maybe you'll end up just like her."

Normally this is where I'd have hollered for Mom or Dad or both of them, but I couldn't. Tess was just—she looked so normal, so Tess-like, but what she was saying—it scared the crap out of me. I didn't want to be haunted.

I didn't want Tess to sound so happy about it.

So I just stood there, staring and scared, until she walked away.

When I finally worked up the nerve to ask Mom about my eyes, she said that yes, they did look like her mother's, and then, "Why do you ask?"

I shrugged.

"You're not like her, though," Mom said, leaning over and smoothing my hair away from my face. "You're like your father. When he decided to be who he really was, when he stood up for himself, he—well, let's just say you can tell he's your dad."

I didn't know exactly what that meant, but didn't ask. I figured it had something to do with Dad's brother, John, who'd died when Dad was in high school, and how Dad had left home for a while afterward. Mostly—after hearing that and what Tess had told me—I decided my parents hardly ever talked about their pasts and their families for a reason.

I still wanted to be Tess, though. I wanted to be able to make people smile like she did, wanted to always know what to say or what to wear. I wanted to have that mysterious something she had, I wanted her ability to make everyone who met her turn to her, like her. I suppose I could have told someone about Tess's moments of darkness, the ones that only happened at home, in private, but my parents never talked about it to anyone and I— well, everyone would have said I was jealous. Younger sisters who aren't as pretty and perfect as their older sisters always are, right?

And the truth is, I was. Those few moments at home aside, Tess was everything you could ever want to be.

Then Claire got pregnant right after the start of her and Tess's senior year and Tess . . . she changed. Not on the surface, not in the glossy self she dressed up every day and that she let everyone see. But at home, in private, she was different. She was silent. She was angry. She was careful to never show it except at home, but at home, being around her was like—it was like being around someone who was so angry they were sick with it.

And I didn't want to be like her anymore.

Sometimes, especially as Claire's pregnancy really started to show and Tess was waiting to hear about college, she'd just lie on her bed and stare at the ceiling. And not just for a little while. For hours.

And once, we ran into Claire and her mother at the grocery store when Mom sent us to get hamburger buns. Tess acted like she didn't see them, but the whole car ride home, all she talked about was how much she hated Claire. She spoke so much and so fast spit flew out of her mouth, dangled from the corner of her lips, and when she ran her hands through her hair, she did it so hard that thick strands of it were wrapped around her fingers when she lifted them away.

That wasn't the worst moment, though. Not for me.

The worst was the summer night I came home after I broke my own heart—and how stupid I'd been back then, at fifteen, to not see that you could do that, to not see that you could destroy yourself more thoroughly than anyone else could—and found Tess sitting in the living room.

She was sitting there, eighteen and golden, and she smiled at me, a real smile, a beautiful, heart-stopping Tess smile, and then said, "Abby? Are you—is something wrong?" her smile fading like she understood how I felt.

"Nothing," I said, wanting to destroy her, the world, everything. As if Tess could ever understand how I felt. As if anything truly bad had ever happened to her.

"Okay," she said slowly, clearly not buying it, and then moved her feet from the sofa to the floor, making space for me. "Want to watch a movie about aliens trying to destroy the world?"

I looked at the television screen. "You're watching that stupid 'modern' version of Cinderella starring the actress whose head weighs more than her whole body for the ten millionth time."

"I know," she said. "But I can change the channel. And hey, you can laugh at me when I get scared."

"I don't want—"

"I know how you feel," she said. "You don't have to tell me, but just—I really do know, okay?"

I didn't believe her—I'd spent my whole life watching her break hearts, not getting hers broken, after all, but she sounded so sincere. That was another thing about Tess. She had this way of making everything and anything sound true, sound like she knew what you meant, that she understood you.

She had a way of making you feel like she needed to be there for you. Like she wanted to. And that night, I needed to believe that someone was there for me.

Even if it was her.

And so I sat next to her, and we watched a movie where people got eaten by aliens. Tess hid her face behind her hands for most of it and never once said a word about the sand on my clothes or how the mascara she'd seen me put on before she left for work had washed into muddy smears under my eyes. She was so nice, so understanding—so Tess. And I hated her for it. For being so perfect yet again.

When I went to bed that night, I lay there, dry-eyed because I wasn't going to cry. I wouldn't let myself, and wondered if Tess would ever know what heartbreak was.

If she would ever know anything unpleasant, and how much I wished that she would.

And now she does.

I know I didn't cause the accident, I know I'm not why Tess's in the hospital. But now I wish I could take all the anger I've ever felt when I looked at Tess, when I thought about her, and make it disappear.

I wish a part of me doesn't still feel that anger when I look at her lying silent and far away. I wish I wanted her to wake up only because I miss her.

But I don't. I miss her, but not like I should. I . . . I want her to wake up so I don't have to be tied to her forever.

I want her to wake up so I won't forever be reminded that I'm not her.

That I'll never be her.

thirteen

"Hello, sunshine," Clement says when I come into the hospital the next day, frowning because my bag got wet on the ferry and the lone bathroom on it was out of paper towels.

I curve my mouth into a huge, fake smile, and he laughs and pulls out a cough drop.

"Found someone to work in the gift shop starting today," he says. "Have something you'd like to say to me?"

I grin at him. "I hear that eating too many of those things you like so much gives you gas."

He laughs. "My wife would have loved you. Do you like Jaffa Cakes? Harriet loved them. Used to be hard to find them over here, but now the supermarkets have international aisles and you can get anything."

"I love them," I say, and wonder what the hell Jaffa Cakes are.

He grins at me. "Now what are you going to do when I bring you a box of them?"

"Tell my parents my new boyfriend is a little older than I am."

Clement laughs so hard he chokes on his cough drop, causing the reception area people to come running with water and offers of help. Sometimes I think he gave more money to the hospital than even rumor says, because normally the people at reception don't and won't move unless someone's bleeding all over the place. Or if it's time for their breaks.

"Go on," he says, waving me off through a sea of faces watching him. "Tell Eli I said hello."

I go up to Tess's unit, and see Eli sitting in the small waiting room outside. He's easy to spot because a couple of nurse's aides are busy organizing carts by the door and gawking at him.

I ask them if they've seen Claire, and they both shrug and go back to gawking. I squeeze past them and into the room where Eli sits, tapping the fingers of one hand against a chair as he stares at the television bolted to the wall.

"Hey," I say, and tell myself the kick-in-the-gut drop I get when he looks at me is just an involuntary reaction. Like stomach cramps after eating bad food.

I don't really believe it.

"Hey," he says, voice as low and steady and sweet as I remember, and the aides out in the hall are gawking so hard I can feel their gazes boring into me.

I can feel them wondering how and why someone like him is talking to someone like me.

"You ready to go?" I say, and they'll stop wondering as soon as Tess wakes up and they see him with her.

"Did you see Clement?"

"Yeah. He says to say hi."

Eli gets up then, unfolding from the chair like a work of art come to life, all grace and skin the color of caramels my mother used to buy, individually wrapped golden candies that she'd melt down and pour onto ice cream.

Tess would eat spoonfuls of the stuff.

"I—you—are you okay?" he says, looking a little hesitant, and I nod, say, "Yeah. Let's go see Tess, you'll love her, trust me," willing my voice not to crack, willing myself to sound normal, like I'm not hoping so hard my heart hurts.

Like I'm not noticing him.

We head out into the hall and I punch in the door code that lets the nurses know someone's waiting to be buzzed in.

"I wanted to say—I wanted to ask about your bag," Eli says. "It looks a little wet. I can get you a towel or something if you need to dry it off."

I shake my head, say no without words, because I can't talk just now.

I don't know what to think about the fact that he even noticed my bag was wet. No one . . . it's been a long time since someone looked at me and saw me.

I wish—

Luckily, before I can finish that dangerous thought, a nurse buzzes us in, and we walk to Tess's room.

Once I've done that and settled into my usual seat, I feel

better. Less thrown by his comment. By him noticing me, even if it was only my bag.

I look at Tess and touch her shoulder, wait for her chest to rise and fall.

It's such a tiny movement, but it's the biggest one she makes. The one that keeps us all coming here. Keeps us all waiting.

"I brought someone to see you," I tell her, and then look at Eli.

He sits down across from me, and I think she's caught him, that he's trapped by her beauty like everyone else is, but then he starts tapping the fingers of one hand against the chair and looks at me like he's waiting for something.

"He's shy," I tell Tess, and then look at him again, widening my eyes so he knows he's supposed to be talking now. "But you heard him the other day, remember? The guy with the voice?"

Eli clears his throat and says, "Hey."

I look at Tess's face. Nothing.

"Can you say something else?" I say.

"Like what?"

"I don't know. Whatever you tell girls when you meet them." I don't know what else to do. Tess talks to guys. I don't. They don't even notice me.

I turn back to Tess and watch her face as he starts to talk.

"Um. I'm Eli," he says. "I go to Saint Andrew's. I'm a junior, and I—"

"A junior?" I say, and look at him again. His fingers are still tapping against the chair. "There's no way you're a junior."

"I am."

Oh, crap. I was sure he was a senior, eighteen and getting ready for college. "You don't look like any of the guys in my school. How old are you?" Maybe he got held back a year or something. Anything.

"Seventeen."

Double crap. "Okay, but you'll be eighteen soon, right?"

"Well, if nine months counts as soon."

I widen my eyes again and then glance at Tess. "Soon, right?"

"Oh. Right," he says.

"You can tell him all about college," I tell Tess. "How to survive his freshman year and all that. And you're really only halfway through your sophomore year, and twenty isn't that much older than eighteen. Plus he's thinking about majoring in English, just like you. If you wake up, the two of you can try to convince me that Shakespeare is interesting, never mind that you can't understand anything the people in his plays say."

"I'm not going to major in English. And I don't get what's so great about Shake—"

I clear my throat then, to get him to stop, and look at him.

He's not even looking at Tess. He's looking at me like I'm some sort of puzzle he can't figure out. Maybe he's overwhelmed by Tess or thinks I'm weird. Or both.

"He's kidding," I tell Tess. "You know how guys are. Remember when you were Juliet during junior year and the understudy put laxatives in Bill Waford's lunch so he'd be the one who'd get to kiss you? And then Bill begged to have the play's run extended so—"

"Did that really happen?" Eli says. He's still tapping his

fingers, but now against his arms. It's like he's playing the piano on his skin or something.

I nod. "Just about every guy in school tried out for Romeo as soon as they found out Tess was auditioning for Juliet."

"What if she hadn't gotten the part?"

"See, now you have to wake up," I tell Tess. "Show him how there's no way anyone else could have gotten it. You were the only one who could ever play a girl people would die for."

"Were you in the play?"

"Huh?" I say, startled.

"The play. Were you in it?"

"Who'd want to see me onstage?" I say. "Plus, because everyone knew Tess was going to try out, they didn't even open the auditions to freshmen."

"So you're a junior now, like me?"

"Yeah," I say, surprised he's figured out what grade I'm in. "But you're clearly way more ready for college and stuff than me."

Eli glances down at his hands, which are still moving, and then blushes.

He even makes embarrassed look good. He doesn't turn bright red or anything, but two spots of color appear right below his cheekbones, making them appear more prominent. Making him look vulnerable, and almost accessible to someone like me.

And he sees me looking. I can tell because he stills for a moment, staring right at me. Damn, damn, damn.

I turn back to Tess, watching her still face.

"Say something else, please," I tell him, because I don't

know what else to say, and I don't want to think about him catching me looking at him.

"Like what?"

"Talk to her like you would if I wasn't here," I say. "Just pretend I'm part of the wall or something." If he acts like I'm invisible, I will be, and then things will be normal again.

He's silent for a moment, and then he says, "I don't know how I'm supposed to pretend your sister is part of the wall, Tess. She's very . . . she's like a dragon, sort of."

That hurts. But I asked him to act like I wasn't there, didn't I? And got called a big scaly fire-breathing monster. Fabulous.

"See?" I tell Tess, and make sure to keep my voice light. "He clearly needs to be protected from me. So wake up, okay?"

Nothing. I pull my knees up to my chest, curling into the chair, and fiddle with the laces on my sneakers.

"Sorry," Eli says.

"Oh, she's just flirting," I say, and force myself to uncurl, to sound unconcerned, but what more does she need? "You'll see when you get to know her. The summer before she went to college, she was working over here, in Organic Gourmet, and guys from Milford would actually ride the ferry over to Ferrisville just to try and get her to talk to them."

Well, one guy. Jack.

"You don't like Organic Gourmet?"

"What do you mean?"

"You made a face when you said it," he says.

I shrug. "That's what us dragons do."

"I didn't mean—"

"It's okay," I tell him. "I know what I look like. What I . . . what I am." As soon as I've said it, I look at Tess again, but she's still unmoving. Still silent.

Still not fully here.

"We should go now," I say, and get up. I force myself to say good-bye to Tess, to not act like how he's gotten me to admit what I am—and how I did it in front of her—has rattled me.

I force myself not to look at him.

Outside her room, I walk out of the unit and head for the elevators. I don't look at him when I say, "Same time tomorrow?"

I expect him to say he doesn't think it's working, that having me sitting there is annoying or weird or both, but he just says, "Okay."

I don't look back when I leave, and I don't think about him on the way home.

I think about what happened the summer before Tess went to college, when she was eighteen and I was fifteen, instead.

I think about Jack.

fourteen

Tess met Jack first.

She'd gotten a scholarship to college of course, not because of her grades but because she "exemplified leadership potential." She got a summer job over in Milford, as a checkout clerk for all the overpriced food at the Organic Gourmet market. (Milford doesn't have things like supermarkets, you see. Just "markets" and "boutiques." Ugh.)

My parents didn't understand—didn't she want to see her friends, didn't she want to have fun, didn't she know college was taken care of?—but she said she wanted to work. She said she was going to save money for books and other things her scholarship didn't cover.

To be honest, I think she got a job because Claire lived so

close to us and because Claire had stopped hiding in her house. Instead, she was starting to walk around her yard, walk around town, showing off Cole and smiling like she'd glimpsed something amazing no one else ever had. I think that was when Tess realized Claire was never going to issue whatever sort of apology Tess was waiting for.

So Tess went to work, and Jack came into Organic Gourmet on Wednesday, June 30th.

I sometimes wonder if I'll always remember that date, and how I felt when I looked up from the book I was reading on the front porch when I heard Tess turn onto our street and saw him walking behind her, shoulders hunched like he was nervous.

And he was. I could tell as soon as I saw him. Jack was cute; tall with sandy hair and wire-rimmed glasses that he was forever shoving up his nose. He had freckles on his cheeks, a broad, quick scattering, and on that first night, as he stood talking to Tess by the steps, I could see the pale underside of his arms sticking out from the T-shirt he wore.

His arms weren't stick-thin or anything, just pale, but the sight of that skin . . . it looked vulnerable, somehow. And that got to me.

He got to me.

He looked nervous. He looked like he needed a hug. And I wanted to be the one to hug him. When I looked at him, he looked like how I felt, unsure but eager, ready to fall in love.

The problem was, of course, that his look was aimed at Tess and not me.

Tess was too nice—and too used to adoration—to blow

him off, so she let him follow her home. Let him talk to her. And so she—and me, because I would sit on the porch and listen to them talk—learned he was going to college to study biology. He wanted to be a doctor, wanted to join a volunteer organization and work overseas. He wanted to help people who wouldn't be helped otherwise. He wanted to be someone.

He never said that he wanted to matter, of course, but I understood how he felt when he talked to Tess about his plans. I didn't want to save the world or anything like that, but I wanted to live and work somewhere where people noticed me. Where I wasn't only "Tess's sister." Where I wasn't a smaller, uglier version of perfection. Where I was just me.

Jack was glad to be done with Saint Andrew's, because he wanted to go to a school where he didn't know everyone, and he hadn't had a girlfriend since the girl he'd been seeing on and off for a few years dumped him right after her school's final formal (Milford schools never had proms, only formals) and then went off to backpack around Europe until she left for college.

Tess never knew any of that stuff. But I did. I asked questions, and he answered them.

That came later, though. First, I had to see him with Tess. I'd wait and watch him walk her home every night, watch him listening to her talk until she'd smile and wave and walk away in this way only she had, a way that left him and everyone smiling and glad to be seen by her. A way that somehow made sure they never noticed that she'd left them.

After about a week of this, though, she'd told him good night and gone inside and he'd stood at the end of our

little driveway, shoulders slumped again, like he'd finally understood what her smiles and waves really meant. That they were
nothing.

His shorts were a little too big for him, and hung down a
little past his knees. The skin under his arms, from his wrists up
to the wide-open sleeves of his T-shirt, glowed pale in the moonlight, and when he turned to walk to the ferry I knew he wasn't
coming back.

I don't know how I knew—maybe the slump of his shoulders matched how I felt, invisible—but I did. I slipped away from
the house and caught up to him.

"I'm Tess's sister," I told him. "Abby."

"I know," he said. "She's told me about you. I don't think
you look like an elf, though."

"An elf?" Tess was always describing me that way, and I
think, in her mind, she was being kind. But did I really look like a
magical creature? Of course not. However, since I was short, and
had my grandmother's unusually colored eyes—well, describing
me as "elf-like," was, for Tess, pretty nice. She always liked the
idea of magical things. Of pretend.

"No, that's not what she said," he said. "I mean, she said—"

"It's okay," I said. "She thinks she's being nice when she says
it. And I bet she told you that you look like an elf too."

He grinned at me even as his shoulder slumped a little more.
"She doesn't date elves, right?"

"She doesn't really date," I said. "She's—I think she has this
perfect guy in mind or something, and he's not—well, who's
perfect?"

"She's just so . . . it's like there's something secret about her," he said. "Something sad, I think."

Tess was about as sad as any extremely popular and beautiful girl could be, which was, of course, not very, but I didn't say that. I liked that he thought there was depth to Tess.

I thought if he could imagine it in her, he would see it was truly in me.

"I can help you with her," I said. "Like I said, I know the kind of guy she's looking for. Do you like poetry?"

He shook his head.

"Well," I said. "You do now."

That first night we talked for an hour, until the last call for the ferry came, the lone whistle from the dock echoing into the night.

Granted, all we'd talked about was Tess, but I'd talked to him, and I floated home, happier than I'd ever been.

I had no luck with guys. Not that there were any in Ferrisville to even want luck with. Oh, there were a few who were cute, but I knew all their fathers and brothers and cousins, and I knew what happened to guys in Ferrisville. They grew up and got a job in the plant. They grew up and grew bellies and lost their hair and sat around scratching their stomachs on the beach in the summer, slowly turning red in the sun.

I wanted more than that.

As for friends, back then I had those. Everyone in school said hello and invited me to their parties and all that stuff. But I had nothing in common with them, and most of my "friends" just wanted to be near Tess, wanted her to notice them and invite them into her world. There were a few that maybe did like me, but they weren't like me.

I wanted to get out of Ferrisville, and they didn't. They might go off to the community college, or even the state college an hour away, but they would come back. No one in their families had ever left town for good, so why would they? People came to Ferrisville and stayed. It might be small, and life might be slow-paced and small too, but nobody but me seemed to mind that.

"Stuck-up," my so-called "friends" said about me when I stopped talking to them that summer. I guess they thought I believed I was too good to talk to them, that I thought I was going to somehow become Tess.

I didn't think I was too good for them, and I knew I wasn't going to be Tess. I didn't want to be. I just wanted a world that was me and Jack and nothing more. I wanted him to be mine and, for a while, I thought he could.

And then, after it was over, I didn't want to go crawling back to my "friends." I didn't want to ask for forgiveness, didn't want to beg to be let back into something I didn't really want any part of. I didn't want to live in Milford, but I didn't want to live in Ferrisville either. I didn't want to hear about boys or clothes or parties or anything. I just wanted to be left alone. And so I was.

And so I am.

But that's now, and I still had to get to that point.

I still had to break my own heart.

In the end, it was easy. Jack kept talking to Tess, kept walking her home. He was volunteering to collect water samples from the Ferrisville side of the river as part of some project the state was doing to see if the water was less full of chemicals than it had been. And I kept talking to him.

He tried to talk to Tess about poetry, and I talked to him about biology, about the latest medical trends, about countries that needed doctors. He asked Tess out to dinner, and when she said no I made him sandwiches that we'd split as we sat in the dark on the beach, talking.

We talked about Tess less after a while, and talked more about him. About me. He was—and will always be—the only guy I ever told the truth about how I sometimes felt when Tess was with me. About how I hated being her shadow.

"You shouldn't think like that," he said to me one night. We were down on the beach, like always, and he pushed his glasses up his nose and turned to look at me, moonlight gilding his hair to a shade that was a richer blond than Tess's could ever be.

"You're not like Tess at all, so why compare yourself? She's beautiful on the outside, but you—you have the . . ." He cleared his throat. "You have the most beautiful soul. I know that sounds stupid, but it's true. Any guy would be lucky to be with you."

How could I not kiss him after he said that?

So I did, and he kissed me back. He dropped the rest of his sandwich, and when we separated he stared at me like he'd never seen me before.

"Abby," he said, and the ferry whistle blew.

"I see what Tess doesn't," I said. "I see you, Jack. And I think you're amazing. Meet me here tomorrow night. Just—just you and me."

"Amazing?" he said. "Me?" He sounded so surprised I had to kiss him again.

And the next night, he took the ferry over earlier, and I slipped out of the house after dinner and met him down on the beach.

My parents didn't ask where I was going or what I was doing. They never worried about me. Tess was the one who got phone calls all the time, who had guys get into fights over her—including a memorable one during my parents' company picnic—and who used to come home way past her curfew, mutely shaking her head when my parents demanded to know where she'd been.

The parties had stopped when she'd quit hanging out with Claire, replaced with her telling us over and over that she had to get into a good school and always followed by long, frequent bouts of sitting in silence in her room. But the guys still called, and people still wanted to see her. My father would some-times joke that it felt like we were all part of "Tess's Messenger Service."

So, no, Mom and Dad didn't worry about me. I was free, free in a way I took for granted. I was free to do what I wanted, to follow my heart.

Free to be an idiot.

And I was one.

The worst part is that I can't blame Jack. He never lied to me. When he showed up that first night to see me and not Tess, he told me he liked me, but that he still had feelings for Tess.

"I just—I think that if she got to know me, she'd like me," he said. "I know that probably sounds dumb, and obviously I like you too since I'm here, but I'm—argh! This all sounded much less stupid in my head."

"But she doesn't want—" I said, and then bit my lip when I saw his shoulders slump. "She doesn't get you. I do. And we're so alike and I—I can talk to you. I like that."

"I can talk to you too," he said, and smiled at me. "You don't want me to learn how to Botox old ladies like my family does."

"Or get face peels." I'd heard Tess mention them to him the last time they'd talked. She was good at diverting guys that way. They'd chase, and she'd send them off to fix themselves up—and then they'd usually end up falling for another girl, one who saw the improved them emerging before Tess did.

"I brought food tonight," Jack told me. "PB&J, with no crusts. Your favorite, right?"

I'd said it was, because he'd said it was his favorite, and so I nodded, pathetically happy that he'd noticed me, that he'd listened to me. When I was done with my sandwich, I kissed a smear of peanut butter off his mouth.

He kissed me back, and I was even happier.

I think it might have ended there—a few nighttime visits, some shared food and commiseration over having feelings for someone who liked you but didn't *like* you—except it was so nice to kiss him. To have him kiss me back. He was everything I'd wanted in a guy—cute, smart, sweet, and I thought . . .

I thought sex would make him love me.

No, that's a lie. I didn't think that. I hoped it, but the bare, honest fact behind what happened is that I wanted to have sex with him. I wanted those pale arms of his wrapped around me;

I wanted to see all of him. I wanted him to see all of me.

He said he didn't think it was a good idea. He said I was only fifteen, and he was eighteen and going away to school and—I'll never forget this—he said, "I don't want to hurt you. I just—I like you too much. I don't want to be the guy you look back on and wish that I'd died a hideous death. And I know you. You'd wish something really hideous on me."

I cried. He still said no.

So the next time I saw him, I gave him Long Island Iced Tea, a drink my mother made only on summer holidays, when she and my father would share a glass and smile at each other in a slow, sleepy way that was sort of cute but also sort of gross.

Jack didn't say sex was a bad idea with a tall glass of that flowing through him, just laughed and said he was drunk, rolling the word around in his mouth, and then added it proved his stepfather right, and that he should have gone to more parties.

"He says I don't know how to drink. Crappy man," he said, and smiled at me so sweetly, so sadly. "That's what he says I'm going to be. What I am. Crappy. Crap."

"Not you," I said, leaning over and cupping his face in my hands, pressing myself against him. "Not ever. You're the best person I know, and I love you."

We had sex on a blanket by the scrubby trees that grow near the beach. He said, "I love you," during.

Except he said, "I love you, Tess."

He froze as soon as he said it, but it was too late. I can still remember how cold I suddenly felt, the wind prickling goose bumps all over my skin. How he pulled away from me and knelt, hunched over and silent, the perfect posture of sorrow.

He said he was sorry, that he was stupid, and that he shouldn't have said it. He said that he knew he'd hurt me, and that he wished he could take it all back.

"They were just words," I said, latching on to his apology. "They don't have to mean—"

"Abby, don't," he said. "I just said I love your sister when you and I—you can't come back from that. You shouldn't want to."

"But I—"

"I don't want to come back from this—be this person I am now," he said. "I can't—I don't want to be that kind of guy. And yet here I am, and I . . .." He handed me my clothes. "I'm so sorry."

I didn't get it. They were just words. I loved him and I knew he liked me. Couldn't that be enough? It was for me.

And when I said that—and I did, to my everlasting shame— he said, "It's not enough for me. I can't—I won't ever love you. Not like . . . not like you want me to. Not like I wish I could."

And that was it. He said he'd come back the next night and he did, sat waiting on the beach, a paper bag in one hand. I hid and watched him until he left.

He forgot the bag, and I waited until I heard the ferry churning over the water before I went over and got it. Inside was a peanut butter and jelly sandwich and a note. Two words.

I'm sorry.

I sat there, feeling the wind blow sand onto me and into my clothes, feeling the night air turn the paper bag damp. I threw the bag into the river—peanut butter couldn't be worse than the chemicals already there—and tore the note into pieces and sprinkled it onto the road as I walked home, watching the tiny bits of paper turn gray and oily as they soaked into the street.

I walked home and watched a movie about the end of the world with Tess. A few days later, she came home from work and said Jack had come in and told her he wanted to know if she'd ever go out with him.

"I felt so trapped, like I had to do something, say something," she said. "There were all these people watching us, and I could tell he wanted me to say yes. I could tell everyone wanted me to say yes because it would be such a cute story to tell their friends and plus he would be happy and everyone else would too, but I just . . . I couldn't. The weird thing was, after I said it, he said, 'I wish I didn't have to know your answer. I wish I didn't even want to ask.' I was like, 'So why did you?'"

Because he'd needed to know.

Because sometimes, you have to break your own heart.

I know Jack didn't want to hurt me. But he did, and all the love I'd felt twisted into hate.

I hated Jack, but I hated myself more. I wanted someone to see me—just me—and want me, and I'd seen it wasn't going to happen. But what had I done? Gone ahead and tried anyway. It was stupid. And I paid for it.

I don't have to worry about that now. I've learned my lesson, and I don't even want to think about trying anything with anyone again. Ever. I just want to be left alone.

And I am.

fifteen

Claire's outside as I pass her house, picking up toys Cole's left in the yard.

"Hey," she says. "Wanna help me pick up this stuff?"

I get off my bike and lean it against her mailbox, then head into her yard.

"Thanks," she says. "I swear, these things multiply. Oh, and tell your mom I said thanks for the coffee, okay? I got called away before I could say it. You'd think I was the only person in the whole damn hospital who knows how to empty a bedpan."

"You had coffee with my mom?" I didn't know Mom talked to Claire. She sure hadn't back when Tess stopped talking to Claire because the one time we drove by her house and Mom waved at Claire when Tess was in the car, Tess wouldn't talk to her for three days.

"Yeah, I ran into her when she and your dad came to see Tess. How's your dad doing, anyway? He seemed—I don't know. Really quiet."

I shrug, because Dad is a pretty quiet guy, plus talking about the hospital had me thinking about my own earlier misadventures. I still didn't get why Eli hadn't talked more. Don't good-looking people love to talk about themselves? Tess sure did, even though she had a way of doing it that made you feel like it was something you wanted.

"Why are you so quiet yourself?" Claire says. "Oh, wait. Your plan. Abby, you didn't really think it would work, did you?"

"It's going to work," I say. "I just—okay, how do you get a guy to talk? What would you ask a guy if you were talking to him? What would Tess ask?"

Claire laughs, but the sound is bitter. "Tess never had to ask—"

"Exactly," I say. "I just thought . . . I thought when he saw her, he'd just start talking. But he didn't, and I don't—I'm not good with this kind of stuff."

Claire laughs, for real this time. "You're full of it, and you know it. You thought the guy would see Tess and say her name and she'd wake up. I hate to break it to you, Abby, but you're as much of a believer in that happily ever after, perfect ending stuff as Tess was."

"Is," I say automatically and Claire looks down at the ground. I hand her the toy I'm holding and add, "And I'm not—you know I'm not like Tess."

Claire takes the toy and lets out a little sigh. "Ask him about himself," she says. "What he likes to eat, does he have a car, does he play sports, whatever. Just ask lots of questions."

"That's it?"

"That's it."

"Okay, I'll try it," I say, and hand her another toy. "I should go home."

"Do you ever wonder what she'd think?" Claire says. "About you and me being friends, I mean?"

"Sometimes," I say, and wave as I get back on my bike.

But I don't. Tess would be furious, and when Claire waves back, I see she knows that too. I wonder if either of us will ever be able to do anything without Tess's shadow looming over us.

That's a question I can't answer.

It's a question I'm afraid to.

sixteen

At home, I race through my homework while I watch television in the living room, finishing it as Mom and Dad get in. Dad heads straight upstairs, pausing only to kiss the top of my head and murmur that he loves me.

"What's wrong with Dad?"

"He's tired," Mom says, and gestures at my books. "How's the homework going?"

I shrug.

"Just like your father," she says. "He barely had to do anything and he made As. Tess was so much more like me, always having to study, always worrying about her grades . . ." She trails off, glancing over her shoulder at Tess's chair at the kitchen table.

"Tess got great grades, Mom."

"Oh, I know," she says, turning back to me. "She just . . . it's so easy for you."

"That's because every decent teacher fled town when the state decided Ferrisville High wasn't meeting even minimum academic standards."

"And not because you're smart?" I make a face at her and she touches my hair. "Your father can't take compliments either."

To be honest, I think I'm about as much like Dad as the moon is like straw, no matter what Mom says. I guess she must see that, though, because she says, "You really are a lot like him, Abby. How smart you are, how determined you are to—" She clears her throat. "You even get upset like he does."

"Dad doesn't get upset." He does, but in a general swearing-at-the-lawn-mower-when-it-won't-start sort of way. There's no way he could ever be like me. He looks like Tess, tall and blond, so how could he? I know things were hard for him, with his brother dying when he was young, but still.

I know Dad doesn't walk around wanting to be seen and then hating himself for it. I know Dad never did anything as dumb as try to get someone who'd never really want him to love him.

"Your father used to be—he was very unhappy after John died. And I know you're angry about Tess now, but—"

Thankfully, the phone rings then, and when she answers it I go upstairs. Angry about Tess?

I wish.

The thing is, I *am* sort of angry at Tess. I mean, why won't she wake up? What is she waiting for? What does she want? I

77

pass Mom and Dad's room and try to be quiet because the door is closed, like Dad has gone to bed, and then walk by Tess's.

I look inside and see all the things she's left on her desk and dresser and floor, things she thought she would be packing up. She hadn't intended to come home to stay. She hadn't intended any of this.

But she hasn't come back either.

"You should wake up," I whisper. "Mom just told me I'm like Dad. I'm not like him. I—" I take a deep breath. "I'm giving you what you want, Tess. I found you a guy, and he's—you should see him. You have to see him. Just open your eyes, and then you can have him."

No reply.

I walk to her desk.

"Have you ever loved anyone?" I ask the pictures on it. Her laptop is there too, plugged in and ready to go.

I look at it and tell myself I'll get Eli to talk tomorrow. I can ask questions. Anyone can do that.

seventeen

Anyone, apparently, except me.

Things start off okay. I get to the hospital and find Eli sitting in the main waiting room, hunched over a notebook, and seeing him I'm struck all over again by . . . well, by him.

He looks up then, of course, and I will myself to not look away, to not act like I care that he's caught me staring at him.

He gets up, slipping his notebook into his bag, and comes over to me. "Hey. How are you?"

"Okay," I mumble. "Ready to see who you've been waiting for?"

He starts to say something, and then just nods.

As we head for the elevators, we pass Clement. He waves at me, then pulls Eli aside to talk to him. Mostly he talks and Eli shrugs, although at one point Eli shakes his head "no" once, hard.

"How are you?" Clement says, turning to me. "Did you take the ferry over?"

"Well, since I still can't walk on water . . ."

He chuckles and pulls out a cough drop. "Harriet used to like to take the ferry. We'd go over and walk along the beach. It reminded her of going to the sea with her family back in England. Of course, her parents never liked the seaside there—they told her it wasn't Jamaica and never would be—but she loved it. She used to buy this horrible-sounding stuff called rock candy when she was a girl. Ever heard of it?"

I shake my head and Clement nods. "Exactly. But she insisted I was the only person in the world who hadn't. Stubborn, stubborn woman." He sighs. "I miss her."

"We should go," Eli says, and Clement looks at him and says, "No harm in missing someone."

"Shouldn't we go?" Eli says to me, a hint of desperation in his voice, and maybe he just wants to get away from Clement and his stories. But maybe he also wants to see Tess.

The thought doesn't quite lift my spirits like it should, so I make myself grin at Clement and say, "He just met Tess and look at him. When she wakes up, you'll never get him to leave her and go back to the gift shop."

Clement looks at Eli, and then back at me, something measured flickering in his gaze. "I suppose the gum will be safe, at least."

I smile and wave good-bye as Eli and I get on the elevator. Eli doesn't do either.

"You shouldn't let Clement bother you," I say. "He's not that bad for an old guy, really. I wonder what his wife looked like. I had no idea she was—"

"What, black?"

"No, the kind of person who'd actually leave Milford and visit Ferrisville," I say, my voice rising. "But thanks for assuming I'm racist."

"I—it's just that everyone in Milford makes a huge deal of acting like it's not a big thing whenever someone who isn't white shows up."

"Oh." I glance at him. "Really?"

"Yeah," he says. "It sucks."

The elevator stops, and the doors open. We get off, and when we're almost at Tess's unit, I turn to him. "I—sorry about yelling at you. And about Milford."

"Me too," he says, and when I nod and start to turn away he stops me, one hand on my arm. He even has beautiful fingernails—not all chewed off or jagged or anything. Mine always look like someone's taken a rusty knife to them. "I—this must be so hard for you. Is there anything I can, you know . . . um, do to help you?"

I nod, acknowledging him but nothing else because if I say anything I am afraid I will start to cry. I turn away, my eyes burning, and start to punch in the code so a nurse will unlock the doors to Tess's unit.

He touches my arm again. "You're using your right hand," he says. "You punched the code in with your left last time."

"So?"

"So shouldn't you—doesn't it feel weird to do it with the wrong hand? Shouldn't you start over?"

"No, it's okay, see?" I say, and open the doors as the buzzer sounds, signaling that we can walk in.

I do, but he doesn't. I glance back over my shoulder.

"Come on," I say. "Tess's waiting for you."

He's got his arms crossed over his chest all tight-like, and he actually looks kind of sick, but he follows me through and heads straight for Tess's room, practically marching behind me.

I sit down, and hear him do the same, but when I glance at him, he's tapping the fingers of one hand against his chair like he did yesterday, only harder and faster, and it's almost as if he's counting or something under his breath too.

"So, Eli," I say, wondering if being around me is somehow really pissing him off before I look back at Tess's closed eyes. "Tell me about yourself."

Nothing. Not from Tess. Or him.

I look at him, and he's still just sitting there tapping away.

"Seriously," I say. "I want to know . . . um." What do I want to know about Eli?

No, not going there. I don't need to know anything about anyone. But what would Tess want to know? What college he wants to go to, what kind of car he drives, and what sports he plays. Easy. And I can always pinch myself to stay awake if he rambles on and on.

Okay, I'll start with sports.

I really mean to do that, but end up saying, "What were you doing when I came into the hospital?" instead, and his fingers pause.

"What?"

"When I came in, I saw you with a notebook. What were you doing?" I say, mentally kicking myself for asking. And for noticing in the first place. And admitting I noticed.

"Oh," he says. "You—I didn't see you."

"Why would you? I wouldn't notice me."

He blinks at me, and his fingers still for a moment. "You wouldn't?"

"No," I say, really regretting my question—and honesty—now. "I mean, I know what there is to see, you know?" My voice cracks a little on the last few words—stupid, so stupid—and I clear my throat. "So, what were you doing?"

His fingers start tapping again but he looks at them like he's seeing them for the first time and then presses his hands flat against the chair arms.

"Drawing," he says quietly. "I was drawing."

"Oh," I say. I hadn't expected that, but it figures. Gorgeous and an artist. "Do you—?" His fingers have started moving again. "What's up with all the tapping?"

He stands up so fast it's like someone's kicked him out of the chair. "I—I just remembered I have to . . . I've got to do this thing for school," he says.

"Oh," I say again. "Okay. But Tess—"

"Tomorrow," he says. "I'll meet you tomorrow." And then he's gone, practically running out of the unit.

"I guess I shouldn't have asked about his drawings," I tell Tess. "Tomorrow I promise I'll ask what you would. I know you want to see him again."

I do too.

Not . . . not that I like Eli or anything, but he's—there's something different about him. Something that seems almost . . . fragile. Like there's a part of him that he wants to keep hidden. That he has to.

I can understand that. I don't want to—not with him, not with anyone—but I do.

I don't tell Tess this. She has to think Eli's perfect. That's what she wants.

But I want to know more about him.

I want something for myself and I lean over and rest my chin on my hands, looking at Tess. Reminding myself why I'm here. Reminding myself why want isn't something I should feel.

eighteen

Dad gets home late that night, long after even
Mom has gotten home from the hospital. I'm still up, sitting in
Tess's room again, looking at all the things she brought home
from college and was going to take back. Laundry, books, some
pictures. Her laptop. Her nice, shiny laptop.

I have a computer, sort of. It's the one Dad got back when
Tess was sixteen. I got it when she went away to college, and by
then it was still sleek-looking but bordering on outdated. Now
it's basically useless, and the hard drive that Tess carefully wiped
clean, her "gift" to me ("It's just like new, almost!") churns whenever I turn it on, and if I open more than one program, it freezes.

Tess had a job at college, filing papers for some archive project the library was doing. The school gave all incoming freshmen

laptops, but Tess saved her money and got a nicer one, and part of me wants it.

I could use it for just a little while, until she wakes up. I could experience being able to write papers without having to save them every ten seconds, look something up online without wondering if the browser will be able to show the whole page.

I turn her computer on, and am met with a password screen. I didn't expect that, but I guess it's something you have to do in college.

I try Tess's birthday: month-day-year.

Nothing.

I try it backward.

Nothing again.

I try her name, then Beth's name and everyone else she'd ever talked about from college, all the guys smiling at her in the pictures she'd brought home.

Still nothing.

"Abby?" Dad says, and I freeze, fingers hovering over the keyboard, but he doesn't ask me anything else, just says, "I was out for a walk. I used to—I haven't gone on a long walk in ages."

He comes over and picks up the pictures lying next to the laptop. "She looks—doesn't Tess look happy?"

I nod, a little frightened by the intense and yet somehow lost look on his face.

"I hope she was," he says, looking down at the pictures.

"Is," I say, and he blinks at me.

"She is happy," I continue. "That's who Tess is. She's happy, she's pretty, and everyone likes being around her. Just look at the photos. She's happy. That's Tess."

"Her fingernails match her outfit," he says, and I look closer, see that they are the same pinky-red as her shirt.

"Just like Mom."

"Just like Mom," he says. "When she was in high school, her best friend, Lauren, would talk about that sometimes, about how Katie always made sure her nails matched her outfits."

"You used to talk about Mom's nails with her best friend? The Lauren Mom talks to all the time?"

"I used to—I dated Lauren," he says quietly. "Back before—well, a long time ago. Before your mom and I really knew each other."

"Oh," I say, because what else can I say? I don't know what's weirder, that Dad went out with Mom's best friend before he dated Mom, or that I'm finding it out now, in the middle of the night.

The fact that Dad dated Mom's best friend is definitely weirder. I mean, Lauren? She's come to visit before, with her husband, Evan, and their kids and everything. And I never even guessed that . . . I mean, Dad? And Lauren? If Tess knew, she'd freak out.

Tess. She'd know what to do now, what to say. Shocked or not—and she would be—she'd appreciate this moment for something, while I—I don't even know what to say.

I settle for "I'm going back to bed," and start to head to my room.

"Did you really see her move her eyes?" Dad asks.

I stop and look back at him.

"Yes."

"So you think—you think she can wake up?"

I nod, surprised he's even asking this. It's not like you can fake a coma, and Tess has so much to live for. The pictures he holds are proof of that, of Tess leading the life she's always had: easy, full. Happy. "Don't you?"

"I'd do anything to have her come back to us."

"I know," I say. "And she will. I mean, this is Tess, Dad."

He smiles, and I slip away, go to bed. I don't sleep though, and it's a long time before Dad leaves Tess's room, almost daylight, and I wonder what he saw in those pictures that had him asking the things he did. I wonder if there are things I'm not seeing.

nineteen

I get to the hospital early the next afternoon because I got out of school early. My last two classes were canceled so we could all sit through an assembly about improving our academic performance, and there was no way I was sticking around for that.

It's too early for Eli to be here, but I look for him anyway. I don't see him, and why should I?

I remind myself of that when I'm disappointed.

If only I could wire my brain to think the way it should, instead of the way it does.

I head up to see Tess, but when I'm buzzed in to the unit I stop, frozen, and stare into Tess's room.

Beth is there. Beth, who hasn't come to see Tess since before classes started up again, and when she left the last time, something about the look on her face, a sort of bitter sadness, made me think she was never coming back. I didn't say anything to anyone about it, but I was right.

Or at least, I thought I was.

"Beth?" I say as I walk into the room.

"Hey, Abby," she says, and moves back from where she was sitting, pushing her chair away from Tess's bed. She's been holding Tess's hand, and I watch as she pulls her fingers away, her thumb smoothing over Tess's as she lets go. Her hair is longer than when I last saw her, down to her shoulders, and chunks of it have been colored a deep, rich purple.

"You don't have to move," I say, sitting down in the other chair. "When did you get here?"

"A little while ago," Beth says. "I wanted—I was just thinking about her yesterday and I thought . . . ." She trails off and touches Tess's hair briefly, like it pains her. "She's gotten so thin."

I look at Tess, at the hollows under her cheekbones, at the frail length of her arms. I don't see anything different, but then I see her all the time. Beth will see things I don't.

"Are you going to stay over? I know my parents would love to see you."

Beth shakes her head. "I don't—no offense, Abby, but I didn't want to see anyone. I just . . . I was cleaning up her room, putting Tess's things into boxes to send back here, and I started thinking about her."

"Wait, send her stuff back? You don't have to do that. She's going to need it—"

"I—I have a new roommate, Abby, and I can't . . . I can't keep Tess's things around."

"Can't? Why?"

Beth's mouth tightens. "Abby, I—I have a life."

"Oh. Okay. Don't let me or Tess keep you then," I say. "When Tess wakes up, I'll be sure to tell her you decided you couldn't be her roommate anymore. That'll be nice to hear, don't you think?"

"I should go," Beth says, and stands up, looks down at Tess with her mouth trembling, and then looks at me. "Look, about me and Tess living together. Before the accident, we talked, and Tess said she was going to move out. We—"

"Hey, I thought you might be here. I came early because I wanted to—oh," Eli says. "I didn't see—Hi," he says to Beth. "I was looking for Abby."

"Hey," I say at the same time Beth says, "Hi," and then turns back to me, saying, "You're bringing guys with you when you visit your sister?"

"He's here to see her," I say. "Unlike her so-called friends, who decide to disappear and then show up and announce 'Oh, hey, I'm getting rid of her things because I don't feel like waiting for her to move back.'"

"Like I said, before the accident, Tess and I—"

"Um, should I come back later?" Eli asks, and that's when I see it. Over the sound of Eli's and Beth's voices, I see Tess.

I see her eyes moving behind her closed eyelids, like a part of her is listening.

"Tess," I say, and lean over, grab her hand. "Tess, I saw that. Come on, open your eyes."

But she doesn't.

twenty

Beth leaves, slipping away when the nurses are
looking at Tess and we're all waiting outside the room. I should
have noticed, but I don't because I am watching Eli, who is standing with his arms folded across his chest again, looking almost as
freaked-out as he did yesterday.

"Do you need to go get a drink or some air or something?" I
ask, and that's when I notice Beth is gone.

"Crap," I say. I hadn't been looking at Eli that much. Or so
I thought. "Beth couldn't even stay and say good-bye to Tess?"

"Is that who was with you?"

"Yeah, her roommate," I say, and notice that under his
crossed arms, Eli is tapping the fingers of both hands against his
shirt. "You don't have to stay, you know. I'm sure Tess is going

to wake up now, and of course you can come back and see her because I know you'll want to, but for now—"

"Yeah," he says. "I'm going—I'll be in the cafeteria."

And then he leaves. Or, more accurately, bolts.

I wait for the nurses to come out. When they do, I'll have to wait for them to call the doctor, and for the doctor to show up, but I have enough money to buy a magazine and I'll read it while I wait and wait and eventually the doctor will come and tell me how long it'll be until Tess opens her eyes for good and how long it'll be until she can sit up. Walk.

Come home.

Unfortunately, none of that happens. The nurses don't see any change in Tess. I explain about her eyes, and I'm told that "emotional upset" can "be stressful for family," and before I know it, I'm walking out of the unit fast, my stomach churning, my eyes burning.

I open the stairwell door, and then, with a sob rising up out of me, take my bag and throw it as hard as I can down the stairs.

Why isn't anyone else seeing what I do? Why? I know I'm only seventeen, but that doesn't make me a liar or stupid or both. I know what I saw.

I wipe my eyes, blinking hard to stop the tears, and head to the cafeteria. Right now, if I go back to Tess's room, I'm afraid I'll scream. Or cry. Or both.

I wonder if my parents will hear about what happened. I know they will. What will they think? Will they think I'm a liar? Be disappointed? Both?

My parents have never been disappointed in me, but if Tess

doesn't wake up, if I become all they have, how will they be able to avoid it? How can they not look at me and think of everything Tess could have done?

How can they not see how obvious it is that I can't ever be her?

I don't want to let them down, but I will. I let myself down so easily, so stupidly, and there is no way I can ever be like Tess. I can't be perfect. I can't make everyone happy. I can't make everyone want to be me.

This shouldn't make me angry, but it does. I don't want to even try to be Tess. I wish she'd just gone back to school after the party. But no, she had to come see my parents again. She wanted to talk to them about her classes, ask for their advice, and thank them for being there for her.

In other words, be the perfect daughter while I skulked around wishing I was anywhere else. I didn't go to any parties on New Year's Eve, went over to Claire's and ate stale microwave popcorn with her while people on television gushed about how next year would be the best one ever and introduced musical acts who lip-synched poorly and exhorted us to "Celebrate!" until I told Claire my New Year's resolution was to never ever say the word "Celebrate!" like it was a command.

I head into the cafeteria, buy a soda from one of the vending machines against the far wall, and pop the top, glancing around the room. Normally I sit by the plastic tree in the corner, watching people look out at the river and silently counting down how long I have until the nurses will be done with whatever they are doing and I can go back to Tess.

I count because if I don't, I could easily get sucked into looking out the window. Into watching the river.

Into getting up, leaving, and never coming back.

The hospital is depressing. It's full of death waiting, just waiting, and Tess's unit is so silent, like the world has gone away, and if I could, I wouldn't ever come here.

I come here—I am here—not because it's the right thing to do, but because I want Tess to be here, really here.

I want her out of this place and back in her life. I want her back at school.

I want life to be like it was after she went to college. I was still in her shadow but not directly under it. Not weighed down by it. Even Tess couldn't fill up Ferrisville from far away. She was a memory. A strong one, but still, just that.

But now she's here, she's a tragedy, and she defines me all over again.

And that's when I see Eli sitting on the other side of the room, looking at me.

I force myself to look right at him even though I don't know what to do when he looks at me. Why is he even looking at all?

He lifts a hand, then waves.

There is hesitation there—I see it and it stings, and I hate myself for that—but he waves.

Run.

That's what I want to do. I want to run and run and run until I am far away from here, from Ferrisville, from everything. I want to run until I can look at myself and not wish I were more like someone I will never be anything like.

I want to run but I know what happens when you pretend things can be different. I held Jack and thought he could love me, but he couldn't. He didn't.

I thought I was free when Tess left for college but now I am tied to her so tightly I am here, spitting and snarling and trying to wake her up.

I am here and once again there is a guy in front of me, a guy who will only ever see Tess, and deep down, in a place I have tried to destroy, part of me sees him and wants. Wants him, wants him to see me.

Stupid. So, so stupid. I square my shoulders and walk over to Eli because I will remind myself why I am here. Why he is here.

I will remind myself that everything is about Tess.

I will remind myself that I'm nothing when put next to her.

twenty-one

"Hey," Eli says when I reach his table. "I—I was going to come back in a little while. I just thought that with everything going on, you might need some space."

I shrug, because I don't know what to do with his kindness. I don't . . . I don't know what to do with someone like him. I don't know why he would even want me to sit with him.

Also, he is looking at me, and away from the fluorescent lights of the hospital, sunlight from outside glinting in and making the river look almost beautiful, he is—it's like time should be frozen around him. I want to trace—touch—his mouth, his neck, and the hidden hollow of his throat peeking out from his shirt.

I think all that—want all that—and it still doesn't capture how he looks.

I'm staring. I know I am. The thing is, he's staring back.

Of course, I am the one gawking at him.

"So," I make myself say as I sit down and drink some of my soda. "Do I have something on my face?"

"No," he says. "I was just thinking about stuff you've said—about all of this. And okay, no offense, but you're kind of . . . it's like I'm not even an actual person to you."

"I think you're a person," I say, stung. "I just . . ." I swallow, because I can't say *You're beautiful and I'm afraid of you.* "I'm sorry I'm not drooling all over you like everyone else must, but I guess I can fix that. How's this?" I arrange my face into a slack-jawed look of awe (sadly, it comes quite easily) and look at him.

"I can't help how I look," he says, like he's got horns growing out of his head or something.

This is making me nervous. He's making me nervous. "Okay, I—I think you're perfect for Tess, and yeah, it's because of how you look. Or it was, before I realized that you're nice too. But you—I mean, you know what you look like. You've seen a mirror before and everything after all, right?"

"Okay," he says, shrugging.

"Okay?"

"Yeah," he says, and then hesitates for a moment. "Are your—are your parents like you too? Do they come visit every day?"

"Yeah," I say, and finish my soda, pushing the can's sides in. "They pretty much live here."

"I haven't seen my parents since last year," he says.

"Oh, so you board at Saint Andrew's?"

"No," he says. "I live here, in Milford. I just—I haven't seen them since . . . it'll be a year in two weeks and one day. They both travel a lot, and thought I should . . . they thought sending me to school here would be good."

"Is it?"

He shrugs. "It's different. Milford is very . . ."

"Scenic?"

"Small," he says. "Milford feels small to me."

I bet he's from L.A. or something. "Where did you live before?"

"Connecticut."

Not what I expected. But then, this whole conversation has been like that, hasn't it? I toss my soda into the trash can near us. "You miss it?"

"Not really," he says. "But at least there people didn't—I get tired of explaining what I am to people here."

"Well, even in Milford, there aren't many people as—I mean, you're like good-looking times a hundred," I say. "When Tess wakes up, she can help you deal with it."

He stares at me.

"I mean the fact that I'm not white," he says. "I get tired of explaining that."

"Oh. I hadn't—I mean, I didn't think . . ."

"You think people here don't care?" Eli says. "They care. Everyone's always, 'Oh, it's so great that Saint Andrew's embraces diversity,' which means, 'Oh my God, there's a non-white boy attending, test scores might slip, and my darling Winthrop might not get into Yale!'"

I laugh because he's right, that is how people over here talk, and when he looks at me, I say, "No, it's not—it's just—that *is* how they talk. Once in a while the school sends their choir over to sing at the town retirement home, and the guys act like walking through town is so daring. Like, 'Look at me! I'm in a place where people don't have numbers after their names!' I just never thought—I mean, I wouldn't think you—"

"I know what you think about me," he says, and for the first time, there's something sharp in his voice.

I swallow, hard, and wonder why there's such a look of confusion and longing in his eyes. Must be about how things are for him here. I can understand that, and take a deep breath. "It really sucks that people are assholes to you. How come you don't tell your parents?"

"My dad grew up here," he says. "So it's not like he didn't know what would happen to me."

"Wait, your dad grew up in Milford? Do you have relatives here? Wait, of course you do. Why don't they tell all the assholes to—?"

"It's . . . complicated," he says. "Have you ever known someone who lived in their own little world?"

"Like, an imaginary one?"

"No, just like—I don't know. The past, basically."

I shake my head.

"Well, that's how my family is. They all want things to be like they used to be."

"I guess I do get that," I say slowly. "I want Tess to wake up because—I mean, I want her to wake up just because, but I also—it's like everyone's life is frozen because Tess is that way."

"You don't like the word 'coma,' do you?" he says.

"I know she's in a coma, I know what the doctor says. But you don't—'coma' is this word without hope, this word that means gone, and Tess isn't gone."

"I didn't mean—"

"Yeah, you did."

He pauses for a moment. "Here's the thing. I . . . I'm half Japanese, part black—and this is what counts in Milford—part white," he says quietly.

"And?"

"And that, just now, was me telling the one person who doesn't care what I am exactly what I am," he says. "It's—you know. You don't like to say 'coma.' I don't like being divided into little pieces of color. And I . . . let's just say I understand what it's like to be angry. But you . . . you're so—"

Horrible. I wait for it, or some word like it.

He swallows.

"Strong," he says very softly. "I think you're strong."

"Strong?" My heart starts to pound, and he nods.

And then he says, "And sad. You're . . . I think you're the saddest person I've ever met. It's like you're drowning in it."

I push away from the table and stand up so fast my chair falls over as I rise. I grab it before it hits the ground, then slam it into the table as I grab my bag.

And then I pretty much race out of the cafeteria. I force myself not to run, but I'm moving fast and my eyes are stinging and I'm angry, I tell myself, I'm leaving because I'm angry.

But I'm not. I'm scared.

I'm scared because he saw me. Because he sees me.

"Abby!"

I hear him behind me, but I ignore him, cutting around a cluster of people waiting by the elevators and heading for the entrance.

When I get outside I force myself to stop. I know he isn't going to follow me. I am not the kind of girl that guys chase, much less guys like Eli.

I'll find him on Monday and I'll just take him straight in to see Tess. No more talking to him.

"Abby," he says right behind me, and to my embarrassment, I jump, I'm so startled.

"Do I look like I want to talk to you?" I say, trying to throw as much anger as I can into my voice, but he came out here, he came after me, and I don't sound very angry at all.

I sound frightened.

"No," he says. "But I—about what I said before, I didn't mean to upset you."

"You didn't upset me."

He looks at me then, and I can tell he knows I'm lying. Hell, I know I'm lying and doing a crappy job of it too.

"Okay, you did upset me," I say. "I don't want or need you feeling sorry for me."

"I don't—"

"Yeah, you do. Drowning in sadness? I look like that to you? Really?"

"Yes."

That's it. One word. He doesn't say it with any sort of force or anger or anything like that. He just says it like it's true and I find myself spinning away from him again.

"No, wait," he says, touching my arm, and I still. "I wish . . . I see what you're doing here. Every day you come and you hope and you—you're so fierce. So determined. And I wish . . . I wish I could be like that."

I force myself to look at him. To say something that makes this about him again because I can't believe he sees things that aren't grubby and awful in me. "So you could go home?"

"So I—so I could do a lot of things," he says, and shoves his hands into his pockets. "Do you . . . do you want me to meet you tomorrow?"

"It's Saturday."

"I know."

"I come at night," I tell him, and I'm not ashamed of having no life, I'm not. Except I haven't ever been somewhere with a guy on a weekend night. (Or day, for that matter.) "My parents come during the day and I come—they let you stay till eight, so I usually come around seven."

"Okay."

"Oh." I can't help it. I didn't think he'd agree. I thought he'd have plans.

But then, Eli is rapidly turning out to be a lot more complicated than I thought he was.

"So I'll meet you in the waiting room by—by where Tess is?" he says, and I nod, then turn around and walk off to the bike rack.

"See you," he says, but I pretend I can't hear him. Not only is Eli more complicated than I thought, he's also a lot more interesting.

He's . . .

No, I tell myself. *No.* He's nothing to me. He's for Tess. She'll wake up. She'll see him. He'll see her. That's all it will take. That's all it ever takes, and then he'll be hers and I'll be . . .

I'll be just fine.

I will.

twenty-two

It doesn't hit me until I see the Ferrisville shore that I never went back to see Tess. I got so caught up in my strange conversation with Eli that I . . .

I forgot about her.

I slink home, where Mom and Dad are waiting for me in the living room like they know what I've done.

Except they don't, because when I come in they both say hello, Mom's voice as warm as ever, but strained, and Dad sounding—and looking—far away.

For all that Mom said I reminded her of him the other day, right now he's reminding me of Tess and how she was when she was out of public view and got upset, right down to how he's staring like he's not here, like we're not here. Like Tess would sometimes do. Like she did when she found out about Claire, or when she came home from college before the accident.

At the time, I figured she was worried about her grades, but now I think about how Beth said Tess was going to move out, and wonder if Tess had lost another friendship, if Beth had done something Tess couldn't bring herself to forgive.

"What's wrong?" I ask Dad, and he blinks like he didn't see me come in even though he'd said hello.

"It's nothing you need to worry about," Mom says, glancing at me before she looks back at Dad, who glares at her so strongly that . . . well, if I were her, I'd smack him.

"Nothing?" I say, my voice rising, and Mom looks back at me.

"Not now, Abby."

"Not now? Are you—?"

"Go upstairs," she says, in her voice that means "no arguing, or else," and I stomp outside instead, slamming the door hard as I go.

Then I sneak over to the living room window, crouching down so they can't see me.

"You know what the doctor said, Dave," Mom says. "It's not—it's not that simple. Tess is—" She breaks off.

"I know," Dad says, and there's silence for a moment.

When Mom talks again, her voice is muffled, like she's leaning into him. "I'm worried about Abby."

I stiffen and press myself against the house, closer to the window.

"Abby?" Dad says. "Why?"

"I don't know," Mom says. "And that's the problem. I looked at her the other night, and she just—she reminded me so much of you when you first came back after John died. She's so—she's so quiet. So angry. So scared. But she hides it, or tries to, and Tess was always so—she was—"

I stand up then. I know what Tess was. So happy. So blah blah blah. So not me.

I head down the driveway and walk to Claire's house. All the lights are off, but Claire is sitting on her front porch, soaking her feet in what looks like a bucket.

"Is that a bucket?" I ask.

"Mom borrowed the footbath she got me for Christmas last week and I haven't seen it since," she says. "My guess is she said she thought it wasn't working right and Daddy took it apart and it's in pieces out back and she can't bring herself to tell me yet." She swishes her feet around in the water. I hear it splashing against the sides of the bucket. I pop open the gate and walk up to where she's sitting.

"What's going on with you and Eli?" she says. "Everyone was talking about how you ran out of the hospital and he followed you."

"It wasn't like that."

"No?"

"Nope. I didn't run. I left. Quickly."

She laughs. "So he did follow you."

"Yeah, but it's not like how you're saying it. We were talking about Tess."

"Oh," she says. "Why?"

"What do you mean, why? What else are we going to talk about?"

"Well, he's beyond cute, for one thing."

"Which is why he's seeing Tess," I say, and she leans back so she's lying down, staring up at her porch ceiling.

"Why does Eli have to be Tess's?"

"You've seen him," I say. "Who else could he belong to? And besides, has anyone who ever saw her decided they'd rather spend time with me instead?"

"I'd rather hang out with you any day."

"Ex–best friends don't count."

Claire laughs again, but the sound is softer now, almost regretful. "That's true."

I sit down and lean back next to her. The inside of the porch is easier to look at than the vast, empty nothing of the night sky. It's real. It's defined. It has a beginning and an end.

"Beth came to see Tess," I say.

"Yeah," Claire says. "I heard. I also heard you got upset."

"Well, yeah. She said that she was boxing up Tess's stuff, and made up some bullshit about how she and Tess had talked before, and that Tess was going to move out. As if Tess wouldn't have mentioned that when she came home."

Claire sits up, and I hear the water slosh as she lifts her feet out of the bucket. "Beth and Tess were—they weren't going to live together anymore?"

"So she says. I think Beth just found a new roommate and wants to get rid of Tess's stuff. What kind of friend is that?"

Claire's silent, and I kick her, lightly. "You're supposed to say, 'A crappy friend.'"

"Poor Tess," Claire says instead, her voice a whisper.

"What does that mean?" I say, sitting up.

"Nothing."

"Claire."

"All right," she says. "I saw—I saw Tess by herself once when she first came home, at the grocery store. She was buying chocolate wafer cookies."

"Oh," I say, because whenever she was really upset, Tess could and would eat enormous quantities of chocolate wafer cookies, the old-fashioned kind that come in a box and crumble if you touch them too hard.

"Yeah," Claire says. "When I saw that, I knew something was wrong. I didn't know it was—I didn't know it was her and Beth fighting."

"You didn't say anything to me."

"I just figured it was Tess being Tess. I figured it was grades. You know how she always—"

"Yeah," I say. "She did—does—worry about them. Poor Tess."

Claire sighs. "Abby, you're dealing with a lot of shit right now. And I know you think Tess waking up will fix it all but it—"

"I know it won't fix everything," I say. "I'm not stupid. But at least then she'll be awake. Be better."

"And you won't be poor Tess's little sister anymore." She looks at me and shrugs. "I was her best friend for years, Abby. I lived in her shadow too."

"Do you ever—do you miss her?" I say.

"No," Claire says, and that one word is so sharp, so final, that I know she's lying.

I let it go though, and just lean back again, looking up at the porch ceiling, at the squares that create it, a simple pattern where everything is neatly arranged. Where there are no open spaces, no gray areas. No places where you can miss someone even though remembering how they were only makes you wish they'd disappear.

Not that I wish that for Tess. Not exactly. I just want her back in her life. I'm tired of mine being all about her.

twenty-three

When I get home Mom is still up, painting her fingernails with her legs curled up under her on the sofa.

"How's Claire?" she asks, like our conversation from before didn't happen. Like Claire is the only person I ever see.

Of course, she pretty much is. Not that it stops me from saying, "What makes you think I was with Claire?" just to see if Mom thinks I actually have a life.

Or could.

"I saw you walk toward her house when you were done listening outside the window," she says. "You know, when I tell you to go upstairs, I don't mean leave the house and then listen to our conversations."

Caught, but I don't care. "What's wrong with Dad? And

why are you talking to the doctor about Tess? Has something changed?"

Mom pauses, the nail polish brush over her last nail. "Your father and I want to know how Tess—how her outlook is."

"And how is it?"

"Nothing's changed."

"Then why was Dad upset?"

Mom carefully paints her last nail, and then caps the bottle. "Because we all are. Look, Abby, I love that you spend so much time with Tess, but you can't—you can't let someone else take over your life, be everything to you. For you. Trust me on that."

I shift, uncomfortable with what she's saying. With how close she's come to the truth: that Tess has taken over my life.

But what Mom doesn't see is that there is no me when Tess is around. That there never has been.

It's not that she and Dad have tried to turn me into Tess or anything like that. But Tess was the pretty one, the special one, the one people loved because she was so sunny and friendly and always knew the right thing to say. And no matter how hard I tried, I could never quite sparkle like she did.

"Are you thinking about what I said?" Mom says, and I nod, watching her eyes. They are calm, collected.

I look at her and almost believe things will be fine.

"I saw Beth today," I say. "I bet the nurses told you, but the reason I got upset is because she told me she's boxing up Tess's stuff. She might as well have said, 'I don't think Tess's ever coming back.'"

"She's boxing up Tess's things?" Mom says, and there, in

her eyes, for a moment, is a flash of what I know she really feels. Surprise.

Worry.

Fear.

"Well, Tess can always move her things back," she says, and she's smiling and calm.

And lying.

I let her, because I know what it's like to need to believe in lies. I once believed I could make someone who loved Tess love me.

I once believed someone could see me, just me. I once thought I could be happy like Tess was.

I know better now.

twenty-four

Dad and Mom are gone to see Tess by the time
I wake up—I like to sleep as late as I can on the weekends. Past
noon is best. Whoever decided high school should start when it's
still basically dark outside should be shot.

I take a long shower and dry my hair, then debate what
to wear to the hospital. Then I get mad at myself for doing that
because Tess doesn't care what I wear and it's not like I'm trying
to impress anyone. Right?

Not that I can imagine impressing Eli, even if I somehow
managed to find an outfit that makes me look both taller and
curvier. I finally throw on an old shirt and jeans that are ratty
around the bottom of the legs because they're too long for
me. (I have yet to own a pair of pants that don't end up drag-

ging along the ground at some point or another.)

Mom and Dad get home late in the afternoon, just as I've finally headed downstairs and am grabbing something to eat. They both look tired and sad, how they always look when they get home from visiting Tess, and especially on the weekends, when I think they remember Tess dragging us all down to the beach or Tess sighing over her homework or Tess getting phone call after phone call or talking to the three or four or twelve people who'd stopped by to say "hi" to her.

"What have you been doing?" Dad says, trying to sound cheerful and failing miserably.

I point at my bowl of cereal.

"You don't have to stay home all the time, you know," he says. "You can go out. If anything . . . if anything happens, we'll find a way to get in touch with you."

I don't say anything, because we both know I don't go out. I didn't when Tess lived here, and I don't now, except to see her.

I finish my food fast and escape to the ferry.

When I get to the hospital, Clement is sitting outside, looking at his watch.

"You look like a little bird," he says when he sees me. "All that hair and those eyes."

"Birds don't have hair, Clement."

"I know that," he says, and sounds almost petulant for a moment, like a little kid, like Cole. "But feathers, hair, it's bascially the same thing. Is it so hard to take a compliment?"

"Thank you for saying I look like a bird," I say, and he shakes his head at me and digs around in his pockets for a cough drop.

"Never loan your car to anyone," he says as he unwraps the cough drop and pops it in his mouth. "You always end up waiting for it to come back."

"You loaned your car to someone?" I didn't know Clement liked anyone in Milford well enough to loan them anything, much less his car.

"I told Eli he could take the car while I was at work," Clement tells me. "But here I am, done with work, and is my car here? No. His father was the same way, only he'd bring the car back with no gas in it. You don't do that, do you?"

"I don't have a car," I tell him, pointing at my bike as I realize what has been right in front of me all along.

Clement is Eli's grandfather. The family here that Eli talked about. The reason why he's working at the hospital.

Talk about missing the obvious. I lock up my bike and tell myself I won't ask Clement where Eli has gone, or what he's done today.

"I'm sure Eli will be here soon," I say instead, which really isn't much better than asking about him because I'm still mentioning him.

"I know," Clement says. "He's meeting you. What did he say to you in the cafeteria, anyway? He wouldn't say anything when I asked him about it."

"He's not meeting me. He's coming to see Tess."

Clement snorts, then chokes on his cough drop. I know I should pound his back, but he feels so frail when I tentatively tap my hand against him that I'm afraid I'm going to snap him in half.

"Damn things," he says, waving my hand away. "I'm always

swallowing them. Harriet got me hooked on them, you know. Nagged and nagged me to give up smoking and finally brought home a box of lozenges that were supposed to help me quit. To this day, I spend more time taking them than I ever did sitting around for ten minutes after dinner with a cigar."

"Wait. You're not eating cough drops? You're eating those things people take to quit smoking?"

"Who eats cough drops?" Clement says. "Do you know what those things taste like?"

"No," I say, folding my arms across my chest. "We don't have them over across the river. We just got chewing gum last year, you know."

Clement grins at me, then glances out into the parking lot and says, "Ah, there's Eli now."

I follow Clement's gaze and see a long, expensive car pull into the lot.

Eli gets out, moving toward us, and I swear I actually shiver inside when I see him coming, this little hot jolt worming its way through me.

Remember Jack, I remind myself.

Remember Tess.

"Sorry," Eli says as he reaches us, handing the keys to Clement. "I got—I was on the phone."

"Is there gas in the car?" Clement says, and Eli grins, then nods.

"Good," Clement says. "Now I can go back to work." And then he heads back into the hospital, leaving me and Eli alone.

"I thought . . . I thought he was leaving," I say, feeling a little awkward about being alone with Eli even though we're in the hospital parking lot and there are a few people around. It's just . . . well, it's the weekend. And Eli is standing next to me.

"He doesn't like being home much," Eli says. "He—he says he gets bored, but I think being there makes him sad." He crosses his arms, tapping the fingers of his right hand against his elbow. "Were you—he didn't say anything while you were waiting, did he?"

"Just that I look like a bird," I say, and Eli stares at me.

"I don't see it either," I tell him, and we head inside.

twenty-five

Claire is in Tess's room when we get there.

"Hey," I say, surprised. "What are you doing here?"

"Someone called in sick, and here I am. You know I'm not turning down extra pay."

I walk over to her and look at Tess. "How is she?"

"I'm just checking her IVs," Claire says. "They're more short-staffed than usual, so I'm making sure no one's running low on anything."

I sit down in my usual chair and Eli comes in then, looking a little worried and hesitant.

"So, you're Eli, who's here to talk to Tess," Claire says, and Eli nods, crossing his arms over his chest. I'm starting to think he's shy. The fidgeting, the whole arm crossing thing—it's all stuff people do when they're nervous.

Claire looks at me, raising one eyebrow like she knows something, and then says, "Well, I've got to get back to work, check more IVs and things. Have fun."

"Bye," Eli says at the same time Claire says, "fun," and that's when I see Tess's eyes move again. Under her closed lids, there is motion, like she's seeing something. Like something—someone—is reaching her.

"Did you see that?" I say, standing up and leaning over Tess, willing her to open her eyes.

"See what?" Claire says, and Eli says, "Yes."

The next few minutes are maddeningly slow. Tess doesn't open her eyes, but the doctor on call is paged, and I sit, impatiently waiting for him.

Claire won't stay, though. She says she didn't see anything.

"I'm sorry," she says, after I've asked her for what feels like the thousandth time. "I wasn't looking at Tess. I was talking to you."

"But—"

"Abby, I really do have to get back to work," she says, and moves past me, not even looking back as she leaves the unit.

"Are you sure you paged the doctor?" I ask the nurse who supposedly made the call, and she says, "I'm sure," her voice filled with something that sounds an awful lot like pity.

I swallow.

As I stand near the nursing station, waiting, Eli is a silent and weirdly reassuring presence. I like that he's not trying to tell me how the doctor will be here soon or anything like that. I glance at him a couple of times and he smiles at me, then goes back to drawing on a piece of paper he must have gotten from one of the nurses.

I walk over to him—not to stand near him, but to see what he's drawing. I know it for the lie it is—I do want to see what he's doing, but I also just want to be near him—and still walk over there anyway.

Eli is not an artist. He's just doodling, like I do sometimes, like lots of people do, squiggly lines and boxes, and it really hits me that he's a guy, past all his beauty, he's a person, and then—

And then, for the first time in almost two years, I want to do something with a guy other than wait for him to go away. I want to touch him. Not in a just-thinking-about-it way, but for real. Not like—not like I did with Jack, I'm not that stupid, I'm not going to pretend I could ever be someone Eli would really want to see—but I want him to hold my hand, tell me without words that everything will be okay. That someone is here with me.

I haven't wanted someone to comfort me in a long time, but I want it now.

"You don't have to wait," I tell Eli, because wanting something and acting on it are two very different things and I trust my heart and body about as much as I believe that the nurse who said she paged the doctor actually paged him.

Which is to say, not much.

"I don't mind," he says, making another box on the right hand side of the paper, then the left.

"The doctor's not going to come."

"He'll come," Eli says.

"No," I say. "No one . . . no one believes me."

Eli stops drawing and looks at me. "I believe you."

I fold my hands into themselves so I won't reach for him. I force myself to think about Tess. About what she needs. "Can you—if you asked Clement, would he be able to get a doctor here?"

Eli shakes his head. "He's not—he doesn't have any real power."

"But he gave all that money—"

"He can't—it doesn't work like that," Eli says, and when I laugh because, hello, of course money does things everywhere, he touches my arm. "People in Milford think he's strange and I don't think—I don't think anyone would even talk to him if it wasn't for the fact that he's, you know."

"Rich."

Eli looks down at his notebook. "Yeah."

I go back to Tess's room. She's lying there, perfectly still like her eyes didn't move, like there wasn't something she was watching behind her closed lids, like there wasn't something she saw with her eyes wide shut.

"Wake up," I say, my voice angry, a whispered hiss, and when she doesn't move I grab her chart—yes, I know I'm not supposed to touch it, and no, I don't care—and write a note about what I saw on the blank back of a card that was once tied to a bunch of flowers blooming brightly in the corner. And then I stick that card on her chart's clipboard.

Those flowers . . . they wilted into nothing ages ago, but my parents have kept the cards, have them waiting for Tess to look at. I figure she won't miss the back of the one that's been signed by Beth, stupid Beth with her boxing up all of Tess's things and her stupid signature, all swooping capital letters like she's some sort of star.

The nurse who paged the doctor comes in then, sees me sticking the card onto Tess's chart, and says, "You need to leave now."

"I'm waiting for the doctor," I say, and she puts her hand on my shoulder.

"Abby," she says, and I'm startled that she knows my name. Almost no one uses it here; I'm just a visitor, I am just Tess's sister. "Sometimes patients move a little. It's not—it's a good sign, of course, but it doesn't mean she's going to wake up tonight."

"I know what I saw."

"You miss her," the nurse says, and I start to laugh because I do miss Tess, but not like she thinks. I'm not the devoted sister, I'm not the noble, plain girl who sacrifices all for her sister to come back. I want Tess to wake up so she'll go away.

I want her back in her life and out of mine.

"Maybe you want to take her somewhere—a walk, maybe?" the nurse says to Eli, like I'm a toddler or dog or just a teenager not worth listening to because Tess isn't moving now.

"Tess," I say, looking at her. *"Please."*

Nothing.

"Can you—?" the nurse says, gesturing at me to Eli, giving him a help-me-out-here look.

"I saw it too," Eli says. "So why can't we wait for the doctor?"

It works. I can't believe it, but it does, and so we wait. Me and him, sitting in Tess's room, on either side of her bed.

It takes me a long time to say it, not because I don't know how, but because I'm afraid to say it.

"Thanks," I get out, after we've sat there for a while, and I was right to be afraid to say it because when he says, "Sure," easily, like it was nothing, I want him to have said something else, and I don't even look at Tess to see if his voice has moved her again. I just—

I'm too busy thinking about how he's moved me.

twenty-six

The doctor doesn't come, and visiting hours end.

I ask if I can wait anyway, knowing I'll be told no.

I am, but the nurse who said she paged the doctor, the one who put her hand on my arm and said "You miss her," like what I feel for Tess is that simple, says, "If the doctor has anything to report, we'll be sure to let you know," as I'm headed out of the unit.

"Thanks again for, you know, before," I tell Eli as we leave the hospital. "See you tomorrow?"

He shakes his head. "Clement and I go to church, and then I have—there's some family stuff."

"Oh, right." Stupid. He just gave up his Saturday night to be here, so why would he want to give up his Sunday too?

"I can meet you on Monday, though," he says. "Regular time?"

I shrug, like I don't care if he shows up or not.

But I am supposed to care. For Tess, at least. So I let myself say, "I know Tess will like that," before I start to walk away.

"Hey, can I—can I take you home?"

I freeze. I don't want to, but I can't help it. No one has ever asked me that before. Jack would sometimes walk me back to the house after we talked, but he never asked, and we both knew he only did it for a chance to see Tess.

I take a deep breath.

"You want to talk about Tess some more or something?" I ask, mostly to remind myself why I'm here, why he's here, but when he says, "Yeah, sure," I feel the bits of me I broke with Jack, those stupid hopeful bits, bleed open.

I feel grubby in his car, my crappy clothes a reminder that I don't belong here. Tess belonged—belongs—in this car. Not me.

"Tess belongs here," I say, and Eli, pulling out of the hospital lot, looks at me like he doesn't understand.

"This is her kind of car," I say. "I can see her in here, you know? She'd like it."

"I don't like it," Eli says. "It's like driving a bus. I used to . . . I used to have my own car. My parents told me I could get a car when I turned sixteen because that's what everyone did, and they wanted—they wanted me to be like everyone else. I was going to get a, you know—"

"Super-fast sports car?" I say. "Let me guess, you wanted a red one too, right?"

"Silver," he says with a quick grin at me. "But we got to the lot and there was this car over in the corner, some car an old lady owned and that her kids had gotten rid of when she died, and it looked so sad. All alone out there, you know? And her kids hadn't even bothered to clean out the glove box. When I looked in it, there was a shopping list. Eggs, bread, tea, all in this tiny, old-lady handwriting. And I kept thinking, What if that's the last thing she ever wrote? What if she'd made the list and put it in the car so she'd remember it when she went out and she never got to go out and just—I don't know."

I stare at him, entranced in spite of myself. "So you didn't get a sports car?"

"Nope," he says. "I got a baby blue sedan with low mileage. It had this huge, soft plastic thing on the gearshift, I guess because the old lady had bad hands or something. When I was upset, I'd pick at it. My parents—" He taps his fingers against the steering wheel. "My parents thought I was crazy."

"So what happened to it?"

"My parents sold it," he says. "Before I came here, they weren't . . . they weren't real happy with me."

"No, I mean, what happened to the shopping list?"

"What?" he says.

"The shopping list. What happened to it?"

"I left it in the glove box," he says. "I didn't want to throw it away. It was her car first, you know? Plus—I don't know. My parents have never done anything like make a shopping list."

"They don't like shopping?"

"They like shopping," Eli says. "But not for food. They have people who do that. Pick out menus, buy the food, and make it. All that stuff."

"Really?"

"Yeah. They don't—they like the house to be run for them. Someone to cook, someone to clean, someone to take care of the laundry."

"Right," I say, like it's no big deal, but inwardly I'm feeling even grubbier. Jack's parents had money but not like this, not money to have someone do all the little things that make a house run for them. "You must miss having all of that."

"No," he says simply. "So, how come you don't drive?"

I wonder what kind of trouble he got into with his parents. A guy who'd buy an old lady's car because her relatives couldn't be bothered to notice that she'd left behind a shopping list didn't really seem like the kind of guy who'd be shipped off to live here.

But then, once upon a time Tess and Claire were such good friends that Tess had talked about the two of them as if they were practically one person, and then she cut Claire out of her heart like she was a stone that needed to be cast aside.

"I don't have a car," I say. "I did, but it was Tess's—she bought it to drive back and forth to school with money she earned working at Organic Gourmet. She gave it to me after her first semester was over, when she decided she didn't need to come home so much, and if she did, she and Beth could—"

"Beth. Is that the—?"

"Yeah," I say. "The girl from before. Anyway, she and Beth came here back then, and Tess left her car. She said I could drive it if I wanted. When I first got my license, every time I went somewhere people would come up to the car and say, 'Tess?' and then look disappointed and try to cover it up when they saw it was only me."

"Every time?"

"Close enough," I say lightly, like the memory of those first few months I had the car, of people asking for Tess and their eyes dimming when they saw me, didn't still sting.

"Why?" he says. "I mean, she's pretty, but I don't get why—you make it sound like you're nothing compared to her."

"I'm not nothing," I say, although I think it's actually pretty accurate. It sounds like self-pity to say it though, and I don't want to start going there. I wallowed in it after Jack, in between my bouts of fury at him and Tess and myself, and what did it get me? Nothing. "I just—one thing about living with someone like Tess is that it makes you face up to things. Even if you don't want to."

It's the closest I've ever come to talking about Jack with anyone but Claire. I don't know how I feel about that. It's strange how easy it is for me to talk to Eli.

It's nice.

Eli's silent for a long moment, and then we turn onto the road that leads to the ferry landing. There are a few cars waiting, parked with their lights on, casting a dim glow into the dark. "So, you still haven't answered my question about why you don't drive."

I swallow, and almost wish he'd asked about the things I've had to face up to, that he'd push me to talk in a way that would lead to Jack. That, I could deflect. This, I can't. It is why I am here. Why he is here with me.

"She was driving my—her—car," I say. "It was New Year's Day, the actual day part. The safe-to-drive-in part. She'd spent the night before at a friend's house, after a party, and she—there was an accident. Her car was totaled and she . . . well, you know the rest."

"So do you think—do you think that if you'd drove that night, you might—?"

"No," I say. "It was an accident. A terrible, tragic accident. If I could have driven the car, I would. I don't—I'm not crazy about my bike." My bike that I used to ride around the summer I fell for Jack. My bike that I put away only to take out when Tess's accident took away my car. My life as I knew it.

"Oh," Eli says, as the ferry blows its horn, signaling that passengers will be loading soon. I get out and motion for him to pop the trunk before I shut the door.

There aren't any cars behind him, but he doesn't start to back up as I move up along beside him, doesn't start to turn and drive away. Instead, he rolls his window down.

"Abby," he says, and I look over at him, breath catching even though I was just in the car with him, even though I have spent all night near him.

"What?" I say, and I'm off-kilter, breathless, because I've spent all this time with him and he keeps talking to me, keeps acting like I'm actually interesting, and it keeps throwing me off. Keeps making me think stupid things like how I could ask him to come on the ferry with me. Come home with me.

I shake my head, but it's too late. I'm shaking.

"Is there anything you're afraid of?" Eli says.

You, I think. I am terrified of you. Of how your kindness makes me like you in spite of myself. Of how you make me dream things I haven't dreamed in forever.

You, I think. But I don't say it.

twenty-seven

My family has breakfast together every Sunday morning. My father makes pancakes, and my mother makes bacon and usually scrambles a few eggs too.

When Tess was younger, she would get out cookie cutters and turn Dad's pancakes into hearts and stars. Sometimes, if she was upset about something, she wouldn't, and a few times, right after she stopped talking to Claire, and then again when she started worrying about college so much she'd basically stopped sleeping, she'd refuse to come down for breakfast at all.

She'd lie in splendid, solitary misery in her room, Mom trying to tempt her downstairs and my father eventually carrying a tray up to her. I'd pick it up later, the food untouched and Tess lying in bed watching the ceiling. She could be poisonous then, responding to my footsteps with icy glares or worse, acting like I wasn't there at all. Looking through me like she looked through Claire.

We kept up the breakfasts after Tess went away to college, although Dad started experimenting with his pancake recipe (the gingerbread ones were a hit, the cornmeal ones—not so much) and Mom switched to turkey bacon and "egg product" after her last doctor's visit.

We kept them up after the accident too, after we knew Tess wasn't coming home right away, though the pancakes had bits of eggshells in them for the first few weeks and Mom tended to forget the bacon until it started to burn.

This morning, Dad's made peanut butter pancakes, and I get out the strawberry jelly and smear it on one, watching it thin and ooze, trickling across my plate.

"You should come see Tess with us today," Mom says, depositing two pieces of turkey bacon on my plate.

"Is this because of what happened last night?"

"What?" Mom says.

"Never mind," I mutter, but it's too late. Mom sits down across from me and says, "Abby," in her tell-me-everything voice.

I tell her, and she glances at Dad as I finish talking, then looks back at me. "We know you want Tess to wake up, and we want that too. But there hasn't been any indication—"

"I know what I saw."

"We—" Dad says, and Mom looks at him, shaking her head slightly.

"She has a right to know, Katie," he says, sitting down with his own plate of pancakes. "We sometimes see—sometimes we see things that look like movement too," Dad says. "I—we saw them more before, back when—back when she was first hurt. But the doctor says she isn't responding, not like you think. Her brain activity is . . . minimal."

"Minimal," I echo, my appetite gone. Tess has been in the hospital long enough for me to learn its language, and minimal brain function means the doctor thinks Tess—the Tess I know, the Tess whose books and clothes are waiting for her upstairs—is gone. The doctor thinks all that's left is a shell.

"We thought you might go with us today because—well, your father and I have decided to transfer Tess to a . . ." Mom presses her hands together, knotting them so her knuckles meet in a straight, white-edged line. "To a long-term-care facility. It's out past Milford, in Oxford Hill."

"What?" I say, stunned, and stare at Dad. "Why?"

He looks down at the table. "Our insurance won't—they have to go with the doctor's assessment, or say they do, and we can't afford to keep her in the hospital for much longer."

"How much longer?" I feel like I can't breathe, but I know I am, I am still speaking.

Still living.

"About a week," Mom says. "Maybe a little longer, but we're not sure. We have to wait for the paperwork for the home to be finalized."

"What if she wakes up?" I say. "No one will be there. She'll be all alone and—"

"She won't be alone," Dad says. "Your mother and I are still going to go see her. That won't change."

"And me? How am I supposed to ride my bike out to Oxford Hill? It's like twenty miles from the ferry, and I can't—" I stop, swallow the words.

I can't say what I want to. I can't say, "I can't do this." I can't say, "I don't want to spend the rest of my life here or in a room with Tess." I can't leave my parents alone when the one person we all know would make a mark on the world is locked inside her own mind.

"I—I'll have to start visiting her with you again," I say. "I can come meet you after you get off work, like I used to."

"No," Dad says.

"No?" Mom and I say at the same time.

"You have school," Dad says. "You need to start thinking about college, about the SATs. You have things you need to do."

"Dave," Mom says. "If she wants to see Tess, we should—"

"I gave up everything to sit by John's side," Dad says. "You—look at what you did for your brothers, for your mother. I don't want that for Abby."

"She's not doing that," Mom says. "She's visiting her sister. She's not—she's not you, Dave. She's not me."

"When's the last time you went out?" Dad asks me, and then looks at Mom. "We both know she doesn't go out, Katie. She goes to school, she goes to the hospital, and she comes home. We let her keep doing that, we keep Abby with us, and before you know it she'll be where you were when you were eighteen. Where I was after John died."

Mom's face pales, but she says, "If she wants to see her sister, I don't think you or I should tell her—"

"Three times a week," Dad says. "That's it. After Tess—after she's moved out of the hospital, that's the most she can go."

"You don't get to decide that. She's not you, David! She's not going to shut down and turn her whole life into one big—"

"She won't spend all her time rattling around the house or at the hospital?" Dad says, cutting her off, and Mom's eyes flash full of something that looks like memory and fear. "She doesn't yell at people when we aren't around, doesn't sit hunched over like she is now, like she's miserable?"

"Stop!" I say.

And then I say it again, louder, my voice echoing in the kitchen, and the words just pour out of me. "She's not—stop talking about Tess like she's gone. Stop talking about her like she's not here. She is here, and she's going to wake up. We can't . . . we just can't think she won't."

Weirdly, Mom's face falls. I'm agreeing with her; I'm telling her that I know I need to be here, that I understand how important Tess is. But she's looking at me like I've hit her.

"Abby, I—honey, Tess isn't going to be the same," she says. "Not ever. You do understand that, right?"

Dad shakes his head at her, like he wants her to stop talking, and I should be happy that he's giving me what I've secretly longed for. That someone, finally, believes I need a life that isn't all about Tess.

I'm not happy.

I'm not happy, because it's like he doesn't believe that Tess can wake up.

Like he doesn't believe she ever will.

"I don't understand you," I tell him, and get up, walk up to my room. I don't slam my door. I close it gently, like Tess would.

No one comes after me. I hear my parents talking. I can't make out what they're saying but hear the murmur of their voices, and when I hear nothing but silence I go back downstairs.

They've left me a note. They've gone to see Tess. They love me. They'll be back soon.

I crumple the note and go back upstairs. I stand in Tess's room.

"Wake up," I say. "Just wake up."

I want to believe that she will. I want to believe that she hears me now, that she hears me when I'm with her. But deep down, I'm afraid she doesn't. Deep down, I don't think she hears me. Deep down, I'm afraid she'll never wake up.

I want her to come back, I do. The thing is, I can't picture it anymore. Not like I used to. What was so sure, so clear, has become hazy.

Has become something I can't quite see.

I don't talk to my parents when they get home. They don't seem to notice, though, because they are clearly angry with each other. So angry they aren't even speaking to each other.

So I am silent, we are silent, and I think about what has happened. What has been said.

And on Monday, after school, I head for the hospital. For Tess.

twenty-eight

I'm in the bathroom on the ferry. It's tiny and stinks, but it has a mirror over the sink and so I'm standing here, holding my breath and combing my hair.

I tell myself I'm not doing it because I'm going to see Eli.

But I am. Of course I am.

He's been the one thing I haven't let myself think about since Sunday morning. My parents and their ongoing silence, I've wondered about all through school. Tess would have known what to say, would have been able to get them talking. She could always get them to, either just by saying "What's wrong?" until they answered, or by having some problem they could step in and fix, some upset that needed soothing. They'd consoled her when she was furious with Claire, and made arrangements to take her to an admissions counselor when she was worried about college.

Tess could fix things now, and I can't.

I'm so tired of knowing that. Of being reminded, over and over again, that I'm not Tess.

But it's not like I get a break. At school, everyone asks about her. People in my classes, teachers, and even the cafeteria workers want to know how she is. I know people are being nice, I know they care, but it's just more reminders of what's happened. Who I am. What I can't do.

And even on the ferry, surrounded by people I know who are going to work, or coming home, or doing who knows what, there are questions. A "How's your sister?" or "Tell your parents we're thinking about them and praying for Tess," or "It seems like just yesterday Tess and I were in the same English class/at a party/ did something amazing and/or fun together. I miss her. Tell her that, will you?"

By the time the ferry docks, I'm beyond ready to get off, like I always am, and I ride to the hospital as if a ghost—a shadow—is chasing me.

I guess, in a lot of ways, one is.

When I get to the hospital, I lock up my bike and go find Eli. I don't look at him at all as we head to Tess's room. I force my mind and heart to see Tess waking up. Picture it: She breathes deep once, twice, and her eyes flutter. They open. She sighs. Smiles.

Sees Eli, and smiles more.

My heart cramps, a painful twist, and I force myself to keep looking. To see what should happen. What will happen.

"I know you'll say that you're fine, but are you all right?" Eli says, and I nod, remembering years of Halloweens with Tess. Remembering how I used to want the same costumes she had until I realized the smiles I got were always fainter versions of the ones she received, that they were sad with knowledge I hadn't quite yet gotten. Smiles that knew I wasn't Tess. Smiles that knew I wasn't ever going to be Tess.

"Sure," I say.

"It's just—I came over here yesterday afternoon," he says. "And I didn't see you."

He was here?

He was looking for me?

"I—I wasn't here yesterday," I say, punching in the code for the unit. "My parents were, though. I guess you met them, right? While you were talking to Tess and everything."

I wonder why they didn't mention it, and then remember how icy silent and tense everything was last night. My parents weren't talking about anything, and they probably assumed Eli had seen Tess and had fallen for her.

That thought hurts more than I want it to.

"No," Eli says. "I just—I was out here, looking for—seeing if you were here, and I saw them through the doors and figured they had to be your parents. Plus you look like your dad."

The buzzer sounds, signaling that we can go in and almost drowning out my startled bark of a laugh. "I look like my dad? Are you sure you were looking in the right room? Because Tess has my dad's hair and his eyes and—"

"Yeah, I'm sure. You both have this—you both have this way

of looking at someone like they're the only person in the world."

"That doesn't sound like me."

"The other night, when you and I were talking, I . . ." He pauses and I stop, looking at him. My heart is pounding.

"What?" I say, and I want it to come out like I don't care, like I'm just asking a question, but my voice is hushed. Hopeful.

"I was thinking it's exactly how you look when you're talking to Tess," he says.

My heart sinks—stupid, so stupid, did I think he was going to say he wanted me to look at him that way?—but I nod like I understand.

I don't, though. First Mom says I act like Dad, and now Eli says I look like him. Or at least can make the same expression.

Does that mean Dad sees Tess like I do? Feels all the things I do? The worry/anger/love?

It's too freaky to think about, and so I push it away, head into Tess's room.

"Hey," I say, plopping into my usual chair. "I'm here. And so is Eli."

"Hey, Tess," he says, and looks at me. I pretend I don't feel his gaze, but I do.

"I . . . uh, I don't have any sisters or brothers," he says. "I used to have a dog, but he had to be put to sleep when I was ten because he had cancer."

That's sad—really sad—and when I look at him and say, "I'm sorry," he smiles.

He smiles and everything—even my toes—goes all trembly.

I clear my throat and look back at Tess. "So, I guess you

and Eli have something else in common—he likes dogs too. Remember how you tried to talk Dad into getting you a puppy after you found out about C—well, back when you were in high school?"

"Oh, I don't want another dog," Eli says. "After having to see—when Harvey died, I—" He rests his hands against the arms of the chair, fingers tapping. "I can't get another dog."

"But maybe one day, you might, right?" I say, pointing at Tess.

"No. I like dogs, but watching someone you love die is—" He clears his throat and looks at me. Really looks at me, straight into my eyes and everything. I force myself to look back and only blow out the breath I'm holding when he glances at Tess.

I force myself to be happy he's looking at her.

"When you love someone you'll do anything for them," Eli says to her. "Right before Harvey died, I slept in the laundry room with him. He wasn't supposed to go anywhere in the house except my room, and even then it was only during the day, but I didn't like to think of him all alone. I wanted . . . I wanted him to get better, just like Abby wants you to."

He takes a deep breath. "Abby really wants you to wake up. I've never seen anybody believe in someone like she believes in you. The nurses all talk about her. How she comes here all the time, how she reads to you. Stuff like that. Supposedly she even yells if someone doesn't come in fast enough when one of your . . . well, when something in here starts beeping. You— you're really lucky, Tess."

Tess's eyes don't move but I'm having to force mine not

to. I'm having to force myself to not look at him, to not stare in amazement at what he's just said.

No one has ever said Tess is lucky to have me. Not ever.

"Oh, now you have to wake up," I tell her, hearing my voice crack a little and hoping Eli doesn't. "You've got to tell him how I used to try and listen to you and Clai—your friends talking when you were still living at home, or about the time I said the person who tried to flush their broccoli down the toilet was you."

"You don't like broccoli?" Eli says, and Tess doesn't move at all.

"No, she does," I say. "Weird, right? When you wake up, Tess, I'll make a whole bunch of it for you and bring it in. You and Eli can eat it."

"Sorry, I can't eat broccoli even for you," Eli says, and I finally glance at him, knowing I should be happy he's caught up in learning about Tess, that he's talking to her like she's here, like she's going to wake up. I'm not, though. Not like I should be.

And when I look at him, he isn't looking at Tess. He's looking at me. He's talking to *me*.

"Tess can be very persuasive," I say, but my voice comes out faint, all flustered-sounding, and when a nurse walks in I let out a breath I hadn't known I was holding and squeak out, "Hi, how are you?"

"I need to check on a machine," the nurse says, pointing at a monitor near Eli. "I think that it's—oh, damn. We need to get a new one of these in here now, and you two need to—" She makes a sweeping motion toward the door.

"What is it?" I say, looking at Tess, trying to see if something's changed, if she looks worse. "Is something wrong?"

"No, no," the nurse says, her voice curt. "I just need to get a new machine in here, and I need you out of here to do it."

I get up, and Eli does too.

"Did I—did I break it?" he asks, but the nurse doesn't reply, is too busy fiddling with the display and gesturing for another nurse to join her.

For all that they sometimes drive me crazy, the nurses here really are pretty impressive, because in just a few seconds me and Eli are maneuvered out of Tess's room and they are clustered around her, faces calm as they move in an intricate dance involving wires and machines and IVs and Tess's still body.

"Well, we can try going back in a while," I say, heading out into the waiting room and flopping onto one of the chairs. There's an old guy sitting in the one closest to the television, head listing to one side as he snores loudly.

I turn to ask Eli if he wants to go somewhere else and see something is wrong with him. Really, really wrong.

He's sitting down too, but his hands are tapping against the chair so fast it's like he's—I don't know. Trying to push his fingers into the chair, or something. And the look on his face . . . it's like he's going to run away screaming, or throw up. Or maybe both.

"Are you all right?" I say, and then remember his question to the nurse. "Hey, you know—you know you didn't mess up that machine, right?"

He nods, but it's stiff, jerky-looking, and then he bolts for the door. I hear what I think might be "Be back," or "Bye," but

BETWEEN HERE AND FOREVER

whatever it is comes out in a rush and is barely audible over the old guy's snoring.

Weird. Maybe he's sick. Or sad. He was just talking about his dog dying, and it hurt me to hear that. Should I try to find him, make sure he's okay?

No. If I do anything, I should find Clement and tell him what's going on. I don't want to get all worked up over what could be wrong with Eli because he's just a guy. He isn't special to me in any way.

Except he is, because I'm an idiot. A full-blown idiot who should know better—and does—but yet still goes looking for Eli anyway.

It doesn't take me long to find him. I head into the stairwell and he's right there, sitting on the step in front of me.

"Hey," I say. "Do you—do you want me to get Clement?"

"No," he says, so strongly it's almost like a shout. "I mean, no. I'm okay."

I know I should say, "All right, see you later," and leave, but I don't.

I stay.

I say, "Are you sure?" and sit down next to him.

"Yeah," he says. "I just—we didn't get buzzed out like we're supposed to, and I started thinking about how I might have taken my first step out of the unit on my right foot and not my left, and then I couldn't stop thinking about how something terrible was going to happen even though I've been trying really hard to not think like that, and—"

"Wait, what?" I say, totally confused.

"I—I have this thing," Eli says. "I . . . sometimes I think things have to be done a certain way and if they aren't I, um—" He breaks off, drumming his fingers against his legs and then curls them into fists, tight ones like he's trying to hold his fingers in. "I get upset and think awful things are going to happen and— oh, hell." He looks at me. "I've got OCD."

twenty-nine

We end up talking on the stairs until it's dark
outside. Eli first started showing signs of obsessive-compulsive
disorder when he started school, and found out he could only do
his work in a certain way.

"And if I didn't," he says, "I'd get—I don't even know how
to describe it. It was like I was going to die—I mean, I actually
felt like I was—and all because I didn't do things like I was supposed to."

It got worse as he got older, and his parents sent him to
doctors, put him on medication, and told him he just had to tell
himself to stop.

"They made it sound like it was so easy," he says. "Like if I
just thought about it enough, I'd realize 'Hey, walking through a

doorway forty times to stop myself from dying if I cross through it on my right foot is stupid!' Like I didn't already know that. I did. I do. I just—I can't help it."

I think about how he walks a little behind me, like he *has* to, and how I'm always catching him moving his fingers like he's restless.

Or counting out something.

I think about how he reacted when I punched in the unit door code with my left hand instead of my right. How weird I thought he was being afterward.

How upset he must have been.

"I—I'm sorry," I say. "I didn't know."

He looks at me. "You didn't?"

I shake my head.

"Wow. I figure it's—I figure it's all anyone can see," he says. "After Harvey was put to sleep, I got even worse. It used to take me two hours to get ready to leave the house every morning. My parents were—they weren't happy. I went to see more doctors, had my medicine adjusted, everything. But nothing—I couldn't get better. Even now, I still have to—" He points at his hands.

"So you came here to see another doctor or something?" I say.

He laughs, but it's a sad, bitter sound. "No. I mean, I do see a doctor. But my parents—I was embarrassing them. All their friends have kids who can, as my father says, control them-selves. But the madder they got, the worse I got, and . . . well, like I said, I was embarrassing them. So they sent me to live with Clement. I spent years listening to my dad complain about this place—we never came to visit, you know, not ever—and they still sent me here."

"That's—your parents suck," I say.

He stares at me.

"I'm sorry, but they do. You're amazing and—" I break off, aware of what I've just said. Out loud. "Anyway, they do suck."

"They're not that—okay, yeah, they do," he says. "I hate it here. Well, not everything. Clement's okay. And you . . ."

I hold my breath, waiting in spite of myself, hoping in spite of myself, but he doesn't finish his sentence, just trails off and taps his fingers against his legs.

"I really hate this," he finally says, looking at his fingers. "I hate my brain. If it worked right my parents would—I don't know. Not act like I was something they need to hide." He looks at me. "What's it like having parents that actually like you?"

"Ask Tess," I say, and realize how bitter I must sound because he tilts his head a little to one side, like I've surprised him. I immediately feel guilty, not just because my parents are amazing compared to his, but also because it's not my parents' fault I'm not Tess. That's nobody's fault.

"I don't mean it like it sounds," I say. "My parents are okay. It's just that since she got hurt, it's . . . I'm not Tess, and it's become this huge, obvious thing that—it's all I can think about. I can't draw everyone to me like she does. I don't know how to shine like she does. She would know what to do now, if I was where she is. She always knows what to do and I . . . don't."

"You seem to be doing okay to me."

"But I'm not. If Tess doesn't wake up in the next few days,

she's getting moved to a home. And my parents . . . it's breaking their hearts, you know? They're not happy and Tess could always get them—or anyone—to stop whatever it was they were doing and focus on her."

"That sounds . . . I don't know. She sounds sort of dramatic," Eli says.

"She wasn't—well, she did know how to get attention," I say. "But you've seen her."

"I have," Eli says. "You're as pretty as she is, you know."

I laugh for real for the first time in ages then, laugh even as my heart kick-thumps inside my chest, a throbbing, hopeful beat.

"Okay," I say when I'm done, and stand up, start to head farther downstairs, outside. "Thanks for that, for being—for being so nice."

"Hey, I meant what I said," he says, getting up and following me, his voice quiet. "How come you're so sure that your sister is better than you?"

"Because she is. She always has been."

"Says who?"

"Everyone."

"Well, I'm not everyone," he says as we walk out of the hospital, and smiles at me.

I smile back. I can't help myself.

I can't help wanting to believe him.

We're both silent as we cross to the bike rack, but as I'm unlocking my bike he says, "Thanks for, you know, listening."

"I like listening to you," I say, and then mentally kick myself. "I mean, it wasn't a big deal."

"It was to me," he says. "You're the only person besides Clement I've told about my OCD. And Clement—well, it's not like he didn't already know."

See, there he goes again, getting to me because he's so—he's so damn sweet. So not pushing back when I try to push him away. "I haven't—you're the only one I've told about Tess. How I can't be like her, I mean."

"Like I said, she sounds . . . dramatic," he says. "You—"

If he says I'm solid or reliable or something like that, I will die.

"You think you're a shadow or something," he says. "Her shadow. But you're not. You shine too. I'll see you tomorrow, okay? I gotta go meet Clement now."

"Okay," I manage to get out and then just stand there, watch him walk back into the hospital.

He thinks I shine.

I think about that all the way home. That, and Tess.

thirty

Tess wasn't—isn't—dramatic. Not really. I mean, she always knew what she wanted and got it no matter what, from good grades to getting into her dream school to making sure nobody talked to Claire once Claire got pregnant, but that wasn't drama. That was will. And Tess had a lot of it.

But as the breeze created by the ferry cutting through the water blows over me, I start thinking about other things. Like how Tess acted when she found out Claire was pregnant. She was mad. And not just in the angry way. It was like she actually went a little crazy. The worst was when she saw Claire walk by our house when she was just starting to show. I don't even remember where Claire was going—she might have just been out walking—but Tess saw her and just . . . snapped. She went over to the fridge, opened it, took out the Crock-Pot of meatballs Mom had made for a week's worth of dinners featuring them, and went outside.

The next thing I knew, Claire was yelling and Dad had raced outside, Mom right behind him. Tess was just standing there, the Crock-Pot lying on the ground and her hands full of squelched meat, red sauce all over them. It's the only time I ever remember Tess acting angry where there was a chance someone outside the house could see her. No one else did but me, my parents . . . and Claire.

She didn't walk by our house after that until Tess had left for college.

But that had been the only time Tess had been "dramatic" in the sense I'm thinking Eli means. I mean, Tess could get quiet or mean sometimes, but then, she put so much pressure on herself. It's like when she freaked out about her grades and how she wasn't valedictorian during the last half of her senior year and went to that stupid admissions counselor.

I was glad Claire was out of school then, so pregnant—and though she's never said it, I think so tired of Tess ruining her life—that she'd dropped out and ended up getting her GED later. Claire was the only person Tess ever—

She was the only person Tess was ever truly cruel to.

But I think that was about Tess being . . . well, Tess. She could be judgmental. Like with guys, for instance. She always found something wrong with them—always. They weren't nice enough, or were immature, or got haircuts she didn't like. And maybe, after years of people doing whatever Tess wanted, Claire got together with Rick after Tess said she shouldn't, and Tess couldn't forgive her for that.

I head home when the ferry docks, exhausted and exhilarated by everything that's happened . . . by Eli. Seeing him, talking to him, and by him saying I shine—and then I stop in the driveway, shocked.

Beth is here.

Mom and Dad are with her, are standing by her car looking perfectly polite—they are both so good at it, and Tess got all of that skill—but I can tell from the way Dad has his hands shoved in his pockets that he's not happy. Mom isn't either, because she's picking at the nail polish on her pinkie finger while she nods at whatever Beth is saying.

Beth is here, and now that I'm not looking at Mom and Dad, I see boxes in her car.

Beth has brought Tess's stuff back.

"Hey," I say, riding up to Beth's car and making sure my bike hits it when I get off. "What's going on?"

"Beth stopped by," Mom says, all casual and calm except for the polish she's shredding off her fingernails.

"Oh," I say, and turn to Beth, pretending I don't see the boxes. "You're going with my parents to see Tess? That's great."

"I was actually telling your parents that I saw Tess—and you—the other day," Beth says. "And that I'm living with someone else now, and she needs to be able to move her stuff in. So, I've—well, I've brought Tess's things back for you."

"For her," I say. "Tess's still here, Beth. You've seen her, remember?"

Beth must have a little bit of a heart after all, because she pales at that.

"I've seen her," she says, her voice quiet. "And I—it breaks my heart. Tess was so vibrant, so beautiful. I thought she'd grow into who she was, but now—" She breaks off, turns to my parents. "We'd already decided we . . . we didn't want to be roommates anymore. I don't know if she told you that or not."

"I—we didn't know," Mom says, and Beth says, "I'm sorry."

"Right," I mutter, and Mom shoots me a quick, warning look. I ignore it.

"You just want to forget about her," I say to Beth even as Mom shoots me another look and Dad puts a hand on my shoulder, trying to comfort and quiet me. "But how can you forget about your best friend?"

"Abby, enough," Mom says. "Go inside."

"What? Beth dropping off Tess's stuff like Tess is gone when she isn't is okay with you?"

"Abby," Dad says. "Go."

"You have no idea what you're talking about," Beth says to me, and then looks at my parents. "God, no wonder Tess was so screwed up. If you two had—"

"Stop. You're saying things you know nothing about," Dad says, his voice very soft but very angry, and then he looks at me. "Abby, this is the last time I'm saying this. Go. Inside. Now."

Okay, then.

I go inside and watch my parents and Beth unload four boxes from Beth's car. That's it. All of Tess's things fit into four boxes.

Four boxes, and now Tess is lying silent in a hospital bed. She deserves more than that. She deserves her life back.

I bang open the front door and head back outside, but it's too late to tell Beth off one last time because she's backing down our driveway and onto the street. It looks like she's wiping her eyes, but if she's that sad for real, she could have stayed, could have gone to see Tess.

She could have not boxed all her stuff up and brought it here like Tess's already gone.

"Well," Mom says, looking at the boxes. "I guess we'd better take these in. I didn't—there's only four of them, Dave. She's twenty and I—how can this be her whole life?"

"Katie," Dad says, helplessness in his voice, and pulls her to him. "These are just things. Her life was so much more than this."

Is. I wait for Mom to correct him.

But she doesn't. She just stands there, leaning against him.

"Is," I finally say, and watch Dad blink at me. "Her life is more than whatever is in these boxes." And then I grab one and take it upstairs.

When I come back down, they haven't picked up any of the others, but they are waiting for me.

"Abby, I don't know if you've really thought about what we've told you about Tess," Mom says. "There's a chance she could come back, but it's small, and her brain is—there's been damage. If Tess does wake up, she won't be the same."

"She'll still be Tess," I say. "She'll still be your daughter, won't she?"

I grab another box and take it upstairs. Mom and Dad don't follow and when I look out at them from the upstairs hallway window they are talking, Dad's bright hair shining like Tess's.

At least they're talking again. They don't look happy, though.

I wish Tess was here. She'd know how to get Mom and Dad inside. What to say to turn them toward her and away from those last boxes.

I can't do it, though. I just watch them and wish I could make everything better. I thought I could but now—

Now I'm not so sure.

thirty-one

I actually go home after school the next day. After last night, with Beth and my parents' reaction to her, and what they said to me, I'm not sure visiting Tess will do any good.

I don't think I'm reaching her.

I'm not sure I ever did.

I'm also not sure I should see Eli anymore. I'm starting to get ideas—I'm starting to wish, to want—and I don't need that.

I figure I'll spend the afternoon watching television, but as I'm walking home, everyone I pass—the mailman shoving an envelope labeled DO NOT BEND into a mailbox, the woman who used to be the office manager at the plant before she retired and Mom got the job, and two no-longer-little kids Tess used to babysit—ask about her.

They all tell me they're thinking about her. That they miss her. That nothing's the same without her smiling face, or "sparkling" eyes, or that she made the best hot chocolate.

I go home, but only to grab money for the ferry. Tess is everywhere and always will be, so why fight it?

I get to the hospital later than usual, of course. I figure Eli will be gone, but instead he's sitting by the bike rack, fingers twitching away on his crossed legs.

"Hey," I say as I pull up to him. "What are you doing out here?"

"I was waiting inside but I—" He points at his hands. "Bad day, with the tapping and stuff, and there was a little kid waiting to see someone and he kept asking me what I was doing and then copying me and—anyway."

He carefully stills his hands, awkwardly forcing them to lie flat. "I also thought—I thought maybe you might not want to see me after I . . . after I told you all that stuff," he says.

"I thought about not coming," I say, and he braces his hands on his knees so hard I can see the tension in them. "But not because of you. I . . . my parents said some stuff last night about Tess. About how—they say she'll never be the same, that her brain is . . . she won't ever be the same."

"Oh. I'm sorry. Are you—are you all right?" he says, and when he does, all the reminders I've chanted to myself, all the things I've sworn I won't forget, they're gone. Just like that. Just because of him.

"I'm okay," I manage to say, and try not to watch him as he gets up.

I do, though, and I'm glad he has to walk a little behind me as we go inside the hospital. It gives me a chance to pull myself together. Or at least pretend I have, because then we get on the elevator and it's crowded and he's right next to me and he smells good, like sunshine and laundry detergent and something else, something that's just him, and I know all about pheromones but never believed in them until now.

Clement gets on at the floor before Tess's and says, "And how are you today?" to me.

"All right," I say, and he glances at Eli. "So, am I allowed to say I'm your grandfather now?"

Eli blushes and folds his arms across his chest. "I never said—" He breaks off, his fingers starting to tap.

Clement looks stricken and then whispers to Eli. I try to pretend I can't hear what they're saying but the elevator is small and Clement isn't exactly quiet.

"I'm sorry I upset you," he says. "I know you didn't say I shouldn't talk to your father, but I assumed it's because of how your father talks about me and—"

"It's fine," Eli says. "I just—my parents always say I . . . I don't want to embarrass you. Okay?"

"Not possible," Clement says, and Eli mumbles something, then races off the elevator when it stops again, for once not waiting until I go first.

"Sorry," he says when I catch up to him. "I—I'm still getting used to the fact that I have a grandfather. Not to mention that I'm living with him."

"Is it bad?"

"That's the thing," Eli says. "He's . . . he's nicer to me than my parents have ever been, and I—I don't know. It's strange."

"Complicated."

"Yeah," he says, and smiles at me.

I smile back—I can't help myself—and start to put in the unit code.

"Hold on," Eli says.

"What?"

"Look," he says, pointing, and I do. I see Claire in Tess's room, moving around, straightening things.

"Oh, it's just Claire," I say. "She works here."

"No, not that. She visits your sister a lot, doesn't she?"

"Right. Works here, remember?" I say, and punch in the code, pulling the doors open as it buzzes.

Claire leaves as we're almost at the room, waving at me and raising her eyebrows just enough that I know she's thinking things about me and Eli. I shake my head at her, and she smiles.

Thankfully, Eli doesn't seem to notice Claire's look, and we settle into Tess's room like we have every other time he's been here.

"Hey," I say to her as I sit down. "Me and Eli are here, and you should probably save him from having to answer whatever dumb questions I can think of."

"Like what?" Eli says.

"Which is better, powder detergent or liquid?" I say, and then stage-whisper to Tess. "See? You've got to help me out here."

"Liquid," Eli says. "My turn. What's better, cornflakes or oatmeal?"

"Ugh, neither. I like anything that goes in the toaster and has frosting on it, or better yet, comes with frosting packets."

"Or waffles," Eli says. "Clement makes only one thing, waffles. But he's really good at it."

I can just see Eli eating waffles now, all sleepy-eyed and dressed in—what would he wear to bed? Boxers?

I mentally shake myself. *Tess.* Think about Tess. "Tess likes waffles. She and Claire used to make the frozen ones and then put ice cream on them." I pause, aware that I've just said a name I know Tess doesn't want to hear.

"Sorry," I whisper to her, and then say, "Eli, what's your idea of a perfect first date?" Oh . . . I just. Great. I know my face must be bright red now because it feels like it's on fire. Why did I ask that?

I know why.

"Not talking about school," Eli says, smiling.

I look at him, hoping my face isn't still bright red, and roll my eyes, then nod in Tess's direction, glancing at her face.

"I actually don't know what my perfect first date is," he says after a moment. "What about you?"

"I don't know either. I've never been on a date. Tess used to talk about hers, though. Going out to dinner, going to the movies, stuff like that." I squeeze Tess's hand gently and tell her, "I know you miss all that."

"Favorite food?" Eli asks, and Tess doesn't move.

"She likes fish sticks," I say, watching her face closely. Still nothing. "Just kidding. She likes spaghetti and meatballs. She has it every year on her birthday."

"So you like fish sticks?"

"Yeah," I mutter. "The best is putting them on a roll with some cheese and mayo and a little lettuce."

"Really? Fish stick sandwiches?"

"What's wrong with that?" I say, and look at him again.

He's watching me, smiling like he likes what he sees, and my whole body, from my head to my feet, feels alive in a way I thought I'd forgotten.

"Nothing," he says. "I just never thought of eating fish sticks that way. You want to have lunch with me tomorrow?"

"What?" I drop Tess's hand, I'm so startled, and it makes this soft, sickening sound when it hits the bed, like it's a thing, like it's not alive. Like it's not her.

I look at her again then, wishing I was a better sister, a smarter person, wishing—as I've always wished—that I could be like Tess. That I could—and would—always know what to do.

"I said, do you want to have lunch with me tomorrow?" Eli says, his face red. "You can come meet me at school. We're allowed to bring a guest if we have enough Saint points and—anyway. Do you want to come?"

"Saint points? For real?"

"Yeah. We get them for showing up on time and stuff."

"Wait, you get points for just going to school?" Rich people really do have it all. I wish I got rewarded for going to school, although the idea of the reward being the chance to bring someone to the cafeteria for mystery meat and limp fries isn't very appealing.

"Pretty much," Eli says. "So . . . will you—do you—you want to come?"

"Why?"

"Why what?"

"Why do you want me to come?"

"Because I . . . we were talking about food and I've got all these stupid Saint points and I figured—I don't know," he mutters. "I just thought you might like to come."

Could he—could he really want me to come eat lunch with him? Like, as a thing? A sort of date-ish thing?

I look at him again and realize I'm crazy. He could have anyone, and he's probably asking me to lunch because—

Because maybe he wants to.

Oh, I hate my brain, but it won't let go of that thought. That hope.

I look at Tess. "Can you see me there?" I ask her. "I'd pull my bike into the parking lot and people would faint in horror."

"Did Tess ever go?" Eli says.

"Sure," I tell him, careful not to look at him, to keep watching Tess. "She dated this one guy for a couple of weeks and he took her to some dinner they have. Remember that, Tess? Mom painted your fingernails for you, and Dad took about a hundred pictures. I can't even remember the guy's name. What was it?"

Nothing, and as I watch her, the silence stretches out, becomes uncomfortable. I glance at Eli and see him looking at me again. This time he looks upset. Almost angry.

Good. I've finally done it. Made him angry, and I bet he's going to leave. I try to ignore the way my insides feel all hollowed out at the thought of not seeing him again, or worse, seeing him here and having him not talk to me, or worse still, say hello and move on like I'm nothing to him.

"Eli, what's wrong with you?" I force myself to say. I try to sound like I'm pissed off, try to say it with challenge in my voice, but it comes out quietly. Sadly.

"You're as bad as everyone who lives in Milford," he says, and it's so not what I'm expecting him to say—it's so not true— that I'm too startled to react at all.

"Yeah," he says when I don't say anything. "You are. You— look, I don't like Milford either, but you act like anyone who lives here is . . . I don't know. Evil or something. Like the fact that I go to Saint Andrew's means you can't ever possibly . . ."

He clears his throat. "Just because I—I can't help that my parents have money, or that Clement does, any more than you can help that Tess is here."

"You can't compare those things! You—you've never had anything bad happen to you or—" I break off as I realize what I've said. How wrong I am.

"I'm sorry," I say. "I shouldn't have said that, but I'm not a snob. Not like you think. I just . . . I don't belong at Saint Andrew's."

"Why? It's just a place, like here or—"

"Like here?"

"Okay," he says, and gives me such a shy, tentative grin that my heart gives a sharp, painfully joyous kick-thump in my chest. "Not exactly like here. Here the gift shop doesn't charge fifty bucks for a coffee mug with a motto on it."

"I bet gum is cheaper, though."

"Not when I was working," he says, and now I smile at him. I can't help it. He's so . . . he should be illegal.

He really should be. He's got me thinking things and wanting things, and looking at him looking at me like he's happy to be doing so, I can't help myself.

I say, "All right, if I do meet you for lunch tomorrow, what time should I meet you? And where?"

And I'm happy. That's the worst part. I'm joyously, stupidly, overwhelmingly happy. I'm not thinking about Tess. I'm not thinking about what I learned when I fell for Jack.

I'm not thinking at all. I'm happy, and I don't care.

thirty-two

Of course, the one time I plan to leave school early
to, well, to do something other than visit Tess, I get caught. Or
at least my guidance counselor, with his shiny, worn pants and
constant cup of coffee in hand, sees me leaving and says, "Abby,
do you have permission to leave early?"

"Of course," I say, because even if I wasn't planning on
leaving, I would now because I don't want to hear about how I
can come see him if I want to "talk," or worse, hear how Tess is
"missed." As if I don't know that already.

As if I could ever forget.

"How's Tess?" he calls out as I'm getting on my bike.
"Everyone misses her, you know."

See?

"I know," I say, and head to the ferry.

I don't get nervous—okay, I don't get really nervous—until I'm off the ferry and in Milford and have biked by the hospital. Saint Andrew's is close by, just a few orderly, overly manicured streets away, but I haven't been anywhere in Milford in ages. Not since—well, not since I came over here to visit Tess back when she was working at Organic Gourmet.

Back when I wanted—hoped—to see Jack. Even if he was watching Tess.

I turn onto the road that leads to Saint Andrew's. It isn't a long one, as the school starts almost right away, its old and clearly expensively kept brick buildings dotted all over the impossibly green lawn. I turn onto a narrow road, following a neatly lettered sign that says PARKING.

There's a bike rack at the far end of the parking lot, forlorn and rusty, and I leave my bike there, wondering if it's stupid to lock it up. I mean, in Ferrisville, or maybe even at the hospital, someone might want to take it, but here? Here my bike looks even worse than the bike rack.

"Hey," I hear, and look over, see Eli.

"Hey," I say. He'd told me he'd meet me in the parking lot yesterday, but my heart's kick-thudding inside my chest anyway, like I'm surprised.

Or happy.

"I wasn't sure—I thought maybe you wouldn't come," he says, and how can someone who looks like him sound unsure? How?

"I'm here," I say, trying—and failing—not to stare.

I can't help it, though. Eli looks like an idealized private-school guy, like a model dressed up in clothes for a brochure, a vision of what guys are supposed to look like but never do.

Standing there looking at him, the sunlight shining onto him and highlighting his hair, his eyes, his face, all of him—I have no idea why he wants me here. I know what the sunlight shows as it shines on me. I am too short, I am scrawny, I am as far from perfect as you can get.

"You ready to go?" he says, and I notice his hands are clenching and unclenching by his sides, fingers flexing like butterfly wings.

He isn't perfect either, and I understand that. I know how it feels.

I put one hand on his arm. "Are you all right?"

It's the first time I've asked anyone other than Tess or my parents or Claire if they're okay in forever, and it staggers me.

But I have to ask. I want to make sure Eli is okay. I . . . I care about him.

"Just the usual," he says. "I'm glad—I'm really glad you came."

My heart kick-thuds in my chest again and I know all the feelings I had on the way here weren't nerves. It was never nerves. It was excitement. Hope.

It's *him*.

I let my hand linger on his arm, feel the warmth of his skin through his shirt, and say, "Me too."

We walk toward what he tells me is the cafeteria. It looks just like all the other fancy, old brick buildings, except there are slightly more windows, as well as tables and chairs outside, and as we head in, I glance at him.

Now that I've gone and done it—touched him (even if it was only on his sleeve) and admitted to myself that I'm glad to be here, that I want to be here—I can admit something else too.

The "deal" I struck with him, the one that was about Tess— it hasn't been about her for a while. I still want her to wake up, but I don't want her to fall for him. I don't want him to fall for her.

I want him to fall for me.

It's weird, but after being so careful for so long, after forcing myself to remember the pain of finally seeing that Jack didn't love me and wasn't ever going to, I'm not scared of how I feel.

I thought I would be, but the truth is I feel like—I feel like I did during those few heady weeks with Jack, when the world seemed like it had a place for me, not as Tess's sister, but as just me, in it.

I'm not saying I want to run around hugging everyone or skipping through fields of flowers, but the hard knot of anger— the one that's lived and breathed across and around my heart— has loosened.

And so my first glimpse of Eli's classmates doesn't make me want to find large rocks and hurl them at their heads, even though I see them eyeing me and writing me off, able to spot my cheap jeans and not-faded-on-purpose shirt for what they are, where they show I'm from.

Eli hasn't written me off. Eli wants me here.

Although, once we're in the cafeteria, he doesn't really look like he wants to be here. He doesn't look upset, exactly, and his fingers aren't twitching, but he looks—he looks like he's holding everything inside himself very still. Like he's willing himself to be calm.

The problem is, it shows. I can see it, in how the fluid grace of his walk is slowed down, stiffened, and in how he keeps looking around. Like he can stop his fingers, but he keeps expecting people to see him doing something they don't want to see anyway.

And then I notice something else. No one talks to him. We've passed by at least twenty guys in their white shirts and khaki pants and acne constellations ranging from a few stars to entire galaxies, and no one has said anything.

Even I get "Hey," at school from people I see in my classes, girls who used to call me "friend" and hang around the house, hoping to talk to Tess until before she went off to college and I drew into myself.

Eli gets nothing, and as we wait in line for food that looks better than anything I've ever seen in Ferrisville High's cafeteria or, frankly, anywhere, I notice that everyone acts as if he isn't even there.

We get our food—and we don't even have to pay, I guess it's part of the tuition—and walk back into the main part of the cafeteria.

It's gorgeous, all windows and light and I think there's even soothing music piped in. It's like a museum or something—at least until you see that everyone is eating normally, the guys furiously shoveling in food just like they do in my school.

It's not that I was feeling like I didn't belong, exactly, but a reminder that guys are guys, even if you give them tablecloths, is a pretty welcome one.

I wait for Eli to make a move to sit down somewhere, but he's just standing there, holding his plate so tightly his fingertips are white with strain, the tips tapping against the bottom over and over.

"Excuse me," a guy says, all sneer, and shoves past me, heading toward a table.

"You might as well leave," he says to Eli as he passes him. "Last thing anyone wants to see is you doing your twitch thing while we're trying to eat. Bad enough having to watch it in class."

Ass. I shift, like I'm turning, and "accidentally" catch my elbow on the guy's plate, sending everything on it flying into him.

"Great, you found a friend as fucked up as you," the guy says, scowling, and then adds, "Retard," in my direction.

I'm ready to match his belligerence head-on, because I don't like how he talked to Eli, to me, but Eli's face has gone from fake calm to a kind of barely controlled rage/sorrow, and it's the sorrow that gets to me. Stops me.

Rage I can handle. Bring it on, slam it into the big ball of anger that fills me up. I can take that. I understand it.

But sorrow—that I have no defense against. Part of why I hated Jack so much the night I realized he was never going to love me was that he really and truly was sorry. He could have kept screwing me and trying to get Tess to notice him, but he didn't want to hurt me.

And that's what broke my heart. Like Tess lying silent in her hospital bed, like the way my parents looked as they stared at the few, slight boxes of her things, the very stillness of sorrow, the soul-deep endlessness of it—it scares me. There is nothing I can do to push it back, to keep it away.

Anger can try to break your heart, but sorrow is what will. What can. What does.

I don't know what to do, though. I don't know how to fix things—Tess's continued stillness is proof of that. I don't know how to make everything all right.

But I have to do something. I look around, see the sea of white shirts—nothing helpful there—and spot a door near a few windows looking out onto the picture-perfect lawn.

"Can we eat outside?" I ask Eli, who nods stiffly, hands still white-knuckled around his plate, and I understand the look on his face.

He looks trapped, helpless and furious, and that's a feeling I know too well. Know how much it hurts. Know how it holds you down, how every day there are a thousand little ways to see there is nothing you can do to change who or what you are.

I walk toward the door, because it's all I can think of to do, and when we're outside, I see an empty table and head for it.

I get there at the same time a slight guy with deep ebony skin does.

"Hey," he says to Eli, and then nods at me.

"Hey," Eli says, and for a moment I think he's not even going to sit down. But he does, and what follows is weird and tense and makes me wonder if maybe all those giddy feelings I'd let myself have before were premature and stupid.

Nobody talks. Eli doesn't talk to me or the guy sitting with us. He just eats his food, one bite after another, with no pleasure on his face. No expression at all really, except a sort of grim determination.

The other guy doesn't talk either, just pulls out a book and starts reading.

I manage to choke down about half the sandwich I'd grabbed, and am wondering if I should bolt for the parking lot when I hear a cheerful voice exclaim, "And this is the Fennelson Building, where our students dine."

I look up and see a bow-tie-wearing middle-aged man who is clearly the Saint Andrew's equivalent of a guidance counselor, because even better clothes can't disguise the "I help students! Really, I do!" attitude that's practically quivering off him.

"Ah, and we have a guest today," he says, smiling at me even as his eyes register dismay at my clearly not-from-Milford clothes. "We do offer our students the chance to bring off-campus guests to lunch, provided they've earned the right to do so via Saint points. It's one of the many things that makes Saint Andrew's so special."

He moves closer to the table. "And, of course, in addition to our dedication to preserving the traditions of a rigorous education, we're also committed to diversity."

The other guy at the table looks up then, smiles fake and furiously at everyone on tour, all white people, I realize, all of whom are nodding like "Oh, yes, of course that's important," as their gazes stray to the other buildings, the other students, or even their watches.

"Never mind that I'm a National Merit Scholar," the guy mutters. "Notice me because I'm black!"

The tour guide/school cheerleader hears enough of that to clear his throat and say, "All right, let's move on to the next building—we've got an excellent science lab here."

"I hate that bullshit," the guy says as the tour group walks away.

"Me too," Eli says, the first thing he's said the whole time we've been here, and I think *Finally!* with an amount of relief that's embarrassing. But I'm still glad he's said something.

The guy doesn't respond, though, just shrugs and swallows the rest of his soda before getting up and walking away.

Eli closes his eyes, like he's endlessly weary. When he doesn't open them after a second, I dare to reach over and touch the edge of one of his hands.

"It's my—it's the OCD," Eli says, his voice quiet. "That's why everyone is—well, you saw it."

Maybe I should pretend I haven't seen what I have, but if Eli feels like I do about his life—and seeing his closed eyes now, I believe he does—the last thing he wants is people bleating platitudes like "Oh, I know things will work out!"

"It's all they notice, right?"

"Yeah," he says, and opens his eyes, truly looks at me for the first time since we stepped into the cafeteria. "So you can see why when you talk about how great things are for me, I—you can see why I don't get it."

"Sorry" seems too small a word to use now, and it's a word

I'm sick of anyway, a word I've heard too many times and I bet he has too. I take a deep breath and look down at my plate.

"It sucks when people look at you and see someone else instead of you."

"It does suck," he says. "Is that how—is that how you think people see you and Tess?"

"It is how people see us. Me. Especially since—" I clear my throat, force myself to look at him. "Since the accident, I know they look at me and see her. See what she's going through, see how—see how my family isn't the same without her. Before, it was just that I wasn't her. Now it's that I'm here and she's not."

I've never said that last bit out loud before. I've never even let myself think it.

But that's how it is, and that's what is at the heart of all the anger and fear I have coiled inside me. I'm here. She's not. And that doesn't seem right to anyone. I can sense it. I see it.

And it makes me something more than angry or afraid.

It makes me sad, so sad.

"You want to get out of here?" Eli says, looking at me, just me, and I let myself see that.

I let myself look back.

I want to leave with him, and so I nod.

And so we do.

thirty-three

After we leave the school, my bike wedged into the backseat of Clement's car, Eli heads into the heart of Milford.

I don't say anything. I like that he hasn't automatically turned to the hospital, to Tess. I like that he asked me to come with him. I like that he wants me with him.

I like him.

I could pretend I don't know where we're going, but if Eli's place in the world is like mine—and lunch at his school showed me that it's maybe even worse, that maybe the only person he has in the whole world is Clement—then I know exactly where we're going.

His home.

I'm right, and Clement's house looks like I thought it would:

large and old, not the biggest house on the block but somehow the most imposing, a certain starkness to its features that's missing from the lushly painted and landscaped houses that are within discreet distance.

"Clement's not much for decoration," Eli says after we've parked and walked into a giant front hall, made all the larger by the absolute absence of anything. It's just a room with a high, airy ceiling, arched emptiness before the rest of the house. "He says Harriet didn't like clutter."

I try not to gape as Eli leads me down a hall with a series of large rooms branching off on either side, but it's kind of hard not to. My parents' house is large by Ferrisville standards—we have an upstairs, instead of the one-floor houses most people have—but it's nothing compared to this.

The hallway ends in a large living room, dark with heavy wood furniture and a massive, deep blue Oriental carpet that sinks halfway up my shoes. Just beyond that I can make out what looks like the kitchen.

"This was my grandmother," Eli says, picking up a photo in a large, silver frame.

A heavy-set woman with nut brown skin and wide, sparkling dark eyes—Eli's eyes—grins at the camera, one arm slung exuberantly around Clement, who is gazing at her as if she's a goddess.

I smile at the photo, because it so fits with everything Clement has ever said about Harriet, with how his love for her still shines in his voice. "She has your eyes. Or I guess you have hers."

"That's what Clement says," he says. "My mother liked to remind my father of that when they were fighting about me."

He hands me another photo, silently. A truly beautiful couple—a tall, elegant man and a tiny, raven-haired woman—are in wedding clothes, smiling at the camera. I can't help but stare at the woman's wedding dress, the train so long it's been swept to one side and then arranged so it pools like water over the steps they're standing on.

"My parents," he says, and I see he has his father's cheekbones, high and sharp, and his mother's hair. There is an intensity about them both, though, a sense of barely contained urgency, that I don't see in Eli.

"No photos of you?" I smile at him.

He shakes his head. "My parents used to send them, but I made Clement move them when I came. I don't like—looking at them just reminds me of how hard I used to try to be what they wanted."

He sees me looking at him and says, "Hold on, I'll show you one." He heads out of the room, and I hear the sounds of his feet on stairs.

After a moment, he returns with a photo and hands it to me.

It's Eli—I can tell that right away—and he's young, maybe three or four. He is smiling at the camera, a hesitant smile, and his hands are clutched tight around a stuffed animal I bet he was supposed to play with, pose with. I think of Cole, with his easy laughter and exuberance, and wonder what could make him look this tense, this anxious.

"You look nervous," I say, and Eli takes the picture back, putting it facedown on an end table.

"I was. My parents were there, and they wanted me to look

179

happy," he says. "And to not 'fidget.' That's what they used to say I did. I 'fidgeted.' It wasn't until my first school asked them to take me to a doctor that they admitted something was wrong with me."

"First school?"

"Yeah," he says, moving away from the picture and sitting down on a long, low-backed sofa.

After a moment, I sit next to him. "So what happened?"

"What did you look like when you were little?" he says, putting his feet up on the coffee table in front of us.

"Same as now," I say, not calling him out on changing the subject. "Only I used to try and—I used to try and dress like Tess. I mean, I've always had to wear her old clothes—" Will that freak him out? No, he doesn't look bothered by it. "But I used to try and make my hair look like hers and stuff. It never worked, obviously."

"And you've always lived here."

"In Ferrisville, yeah."

"Is it really that different than Milford?"

I place my feet next to his on the coffee table. I point at his shiny, expensive shoes, dark leather that looks buttery-soft. Then I point at my own used-to-be-white-but-are-now-dingy-gray canvas sneakers.

"I have sneakers too."

"And I bet you didn't buy them out of a bin where they were tagged 'Buy One Pair, Get One Pair Free.'"

"My parents do have money," he says, a bitter little laugh escaping. "Couldn't have been sent to all the schools I was without that."

"How many schools?"

"A lot. A dozen, at least." He holds his hands out toward me briefly. "And all because of these. Well, these and my fucked up brain."

"You shouldn't—you aren't like that," I say. "I didn't even notice you had OCD until you told me."

"Right."

"Really," I say. "I thought you were nervous around Tess because she's so . . . well, because she's Tess and she's beautiful."

He's silent for a moment.

"I don't really know how to say this," he finally says. "So, um, don't get mad, okay?" He bites his lips, folds his arms across his chest, and then slowly unfolds them. "I just—I don't see what's so great about her."

"That's because she's asleep. If Tess was awake you'd see. She's the kind of person everyone wants to look at. Like you."

"Are you kidding? I got asked to leave my last school because I was taking so long getting ready to work—I had to sharpen my pencil a certain number of times, and then I had to have all my papers lined up along the right edge of the desk and—anyway, there was a lot of stuff I had to do, and I wasn't getting any work done. And yeah, people looked at me then, and at every other school I've been to, but not like how you think."

I'm sure I don't make a face but I guess I do because he grins at me and says, "I swear! Not until I came here, and you must have noticed that it's stopped. Word of my—of who I am, of my . . . you know—it's gotten around."

"Like you've never ever met a girl who doesn't care?" I say, and I know I'm making a face now. I mean, yes, I know he has

OCD, but he's also acting like he's a troll and I'm sure we both know he isn't.

He's silent for a second, and then looks out the window that shows the gleaming, green front lawn. "Did Tess like it when guys wanted her because of how she looked?"

And when I don't say anything because he's right, Tess knew she was good-looking but always avoided the guys who only saw that, he says, "Exactly. Is it so weird that I want someone who actually likes me even when I'm not—even when I can't—" He blows out a breath. "I want someone who doesn't care that I have to walk through doors a certain way and stuff."

"Okay, I get that," I say. "But you're still acting like you're a diseased yak or something and—"

"A yak?" he says, smiling.

"Yeah," I say, grinning back. "And you're not. I mean, who doesn't have problems? So that's why I find it hard to believe that you're having to wander around girl-less."

"Well, you're here with me."

"Like I count. You know what I mean."

"Sure," he says. "At the all-male schools my parents sent me to, there were girls everywhere. Hidden in the walls and stuff. Don't know how I keep missing them. And how come you don't count?"

"Because I don't," I tell him, my stomach fluttering because I think I could count with him, and I definitely know I want to. "You're just being nice, and it's sweet, but you don't have to do it. I know you never would have noticed me if I hadn't asked you about Tess."

"Okay, you're right, I never noticed you before you came in to talk to me," he says, and my heart sinks. I didn't want to be right, but I guess I am.

"I mean, Clement mentioned you, but I was too busy trying to get through each shift in the gift shop without counting all the magazines," he continues. "That's why I was giving away all that gum. To try and stop myself from counting. But then you came in, and you were so intense and—well, a little strange, but I liked that. And then I got to know you, and it's been the best thing that's happened to me here. Or ever, really."

"A little strange?" I'm trying to sound like I'm calm, like I'm just having a simple, relaxing time hanging out with him but:

I never hang out with anyone except Claire.

Eli and I are sitting awfully close now.

Despite what Eli seems to think, I'm not immune to how he looks, and when you combine that with how nice he is, you get—

You get want. And right now, I want to push Eli down onto the sofa or, better yet, have him push me down onto the sofa.

"Abby," he says, and no one, not even Jack, has ever said my name like that, like it's beautiful, like it holds want. Like it *is* want. I can't quite catch my breath, the kick-thud of my heart swooping down into my stomach, breathless anticipation because I know he is going to kiss me; I see the same shock I'm feeling all over his face, surprise at how strong feelings you've told yourself you don't get to have can be.

He moves closer still, so close I have to close my eyes because I'm dizzy with the idea that there's no space between where I end and he begins, and I feel it, the softest, gentlest brush of his mouth across mine, an almost kiss, a testing, and I curl myself toward him, wanting no space between us at all, anywhere, and—

And Clement says, "Eli, there you are! You never showed up at the hospital, so I got a ride home with Dr. Henry, who asked if we got that stupid ham he sent, as if that's going to convince me to let him cut down the tree Harriet planted when we moved in because it's 'blocking his view.' I ask you, who would even want twenty pounds of ham? And who thinks an enormous ham is the perfect gift for—oh, Abby! Hello!"

He steps over to the sofa, gently clapping me on the shoulder. "I was wondering where you were too since I didn't see you come in to visit Tess. I don't suppose you'd like a ham sandwich, would you? We have plenty of ham, don't we, Eli?"

"Yeah," Eli mumbles, and Clement says, "Let's go into the kitchen, shall we?" and waits, smiling at me, as Eli stands up, hands shoved into his pockets, and follows him into the kitchen.

Clement knows what's going on. Or what was almost going on. And the web I was caught up in, the web of being with Eli, of knowing he wanted to be with me—it's been shredded.

Because who did I forget while I was thinking about nothing but myself and what I want?

Tess.

thirty-four

I want to sneak out, but I don't want to be rude to Clement. And I don't—I don't want Eli to think I don't want to be here. Because I do.

That's the whole problem. I do want to be here. I want. And I've tried—I've tried so hard not to do that.

"I have to go," I say, sticking my head into the kitchen. Clement is slicing an enormous ham as Eli stands next to him, a faint, dark flush across his face as he fiddles with a loaf of bread.

"Are you sure?" Clement says, looking at me closely enough that I get nervous and give him my usual angry smile, all bared teeth. He smiles back and keeps looking, like he knows what I'm thinking. How I'm feeling. Next to him, Eli casts one quick look at me, and then returns to staring at the bread.

"At least let me make you a sandwich," Clement says, motioning for me to come into the kitchen. "Eli and I have eaten enough ham to last us a thousand years."

"That's okay. I'm not really hungry, and I—with the ferry and stuff, I have to get there, so . . ."

"Oh," Clement says, sounding surprised. "Well, let me and Eli walk you out, all right?"

I nod, a little worried about what saying good-bye to Eli might be like, but it turns out I don't get a chance to talk to him at all because Clement actually does walk me to the door, chatting about the hospital as Eli trails behind him.

"See you tomorrow?" Clement asks, patting my arm, and when I nod again, he says, "Good. I'll look for you. I'm working at the information desk because Phoebe Van Worley's gone off to see her daughter, who just had a baby."

I look back after I walk out and the last thing I see is Eli peering at me over Clement's head—he's taller than Clement is—a tentative smile on his face.

I smile back, but remember how I forgot Tess as soon as I've taken my bike out of Clement's car. I head into Milford and pass the hospital feeling terrible, but it's too late to stop now. If I do, I'll see my parents, and I can't bear the idea of sitting there watching them watch Tess.

I can't bear for them to know that I haven't seen her today.

I ride down to the ferry, and see Claire three cars up. I'm not in the mood to talk to anyone, though, and don't ride up to her after we've all boarded.

Instead, I sit on my bike listening to the brisk slap of the water against the ferry, and as we leave Milford I head up to the front of the boat to watch it, weaving around Claire's car.

I'm not thinking about the water, though. I'm not even thinking about Tess.

I'm thinking about Eli, and how we almost kissed.

Is it a good thing that we didn't? The sensible part of me says yes. Putting aside the Tess thing, which I can't, of course I can't, there's the fact that I—

I can't think of anything to go there other than that I'm scared. I don't want what happened with Jack to happen to me again. I don't want to fall and break my own heart.

"I know what you're thinking about," Claire says.

I turn, startled, and see she's standing right next to me.

"You didn't come in today," she says, and smiles at me. "Where were you?"

I shrug.

"Clement was looking for someone too," she says, still smiling. "I heard him asking about Eli—guess he wasn't around either. I wonder where he was?"

I shake my head at her. "That's what you've got? You have to get better at this if you ever want Cole to talk to you once he's past, say, six."

"You were with Eli, weren't you?" Claire singsongs, and when I flush, says, "I knew it! Tell me everything, with many details, as I have no life."

"There's nothing to tell. I saw him, we talked, and now I'm here talking to you."

"Saw him where?" she says. "And you should hear how you

said 'talked.'" She drops her voice down on the last word, filling it with innuendo.

"It wasn't a big deal."

"Which means it was."

"Claire."

"Abby," she echoes back at me, and then nudges me with her elbow until I look at her.

"What?" I say.

"You deserve to be happy, you know," she says. "I know everything's changed because of Tess, but it doesn't mean you have to stop living. Just because she's not—"

"Don't say 'not here.' She is here. You see her almost every day. Just because she isn't awake doesn't mean—"

"That's not what I was going to say," Claire says. "What I was going to say is that just because Tess isn't able to go back to her life right now, you don't have to give up yours."

"Nothing to give up," I say, forcing my voice to sound light, like what we're talking about means nothing to me. "I just spent a couple of hours with a guy. It's not a big deal. It's not like I mean anything to him. I mean, you've seen him. He could have anyone."

Claire shrugs. "Okay."

I sigh, because I know what her "okay" means. "Okay what?"

"Nothing. Just—well, people who can have anyone still have to pick someone. And why can't that someone be you?"

I gesture at myself. "You think there's going to be a run on short, scrawny girls?"

"I'm no Tess either," Claire says, "but once someone loved me."

"Yeah, but you and Rick didn't work out."

She blinks, then nods and says, "But you don't know it won't work out with Eli. And stop trying to change the subject. Tell me more about today."

So I tell her a little bit about going to Saint Andrew's, skimming over the cafeteria stuff, which I feel belongs to Eli, is his story to tell if he chooses.

And Eli chose to share his story with me.

"Okay, you're smiling, but you've stopped talking," Claire says. "So you left the school and—wait, I know. You went to his house, right?"

"Yes," I say, and when she makes a go-on motion I shake my head at her. "Nothing happened."

"Oh, you lie. I can tell from the way you're—holy shit, you're blushing!"

"Shut up," I mutter, and she laughs, saying, "So, you're at his house and then . . ."

"I was at his house for a while and then I left. That's it."

"Abby . . ."

"Really, that's all, I swear," I say. "I mean, we almost sort of kissed . . ."

Claire throws both arms up in a victory sign until I elbow her and say, "Quit it. It's not a big deal."

"The fact that it took me this long to get you to tell me that means it's a huge deal. And I meant what I said before, you know. You deserve to be happy."

I want to believe her. I desperately want to believe her—in fact, I want to beg her to tell me again—so I change the subject. "Did you see my parents today?"

"No, they weren't there when I left. Why? Do you think they'll find out you weren't at the hospital? Would they—do they make you see Tess every day?"

"No," I say. "Nothing like that. It's just . . . I hope they're okay. Yesterday Beth dropped all of Tess's stuff off, just drove up with it in boxes and then left. She says Tess said she was going to move out, and she's living with someone else now, but how hard is it to hold on to your roommate's things? Especially when it's someone you've lived with for . . ." I trail off, something about everything I've just said making my head spin.

"Well, maybe her dorm room is small?"

"They had an apartment," I say absently. "Tess said she and Beth wanted more space, so they moved off campus together after their freshman year."

And that's when it hits me. What Beth was trying to say about why she and Tess had decided to stop living together when I saw her in the hospital. How I saw Beth touching Tess's hair, and the look on her face when she did.

The way she looked at Tess when she thought there was no one around to see. The sadness.

The love.

Beth and Tess weren't roommates. Beth and Tess were living together. I think of all the times Tess came home, and how Beth was almost always with her. I think of all the pictures Tess had, all those guys. And always, in every single picture, Beth was there holding the camera. Beth, who Tess was really looking at.

Beth and Tess were together.

"Holy shit," I breathe.

"What?" Claire says, and I tell her. Her eyes go wide, but I can't quite read the expression in them.

"Did you know?" I ask, but I don't get to hear her answer because the ferry docks and we all have to go back to our cars. Or, in my case, bike.

I think Claire will wait for me when I get off the ferry, drive me home so we can talk more about what I've just realized, but she doesn't.

I'm not that surprised, though. If I'm shocked, she must be . . . I can't even imagine what she must feel. Tess, with her endless string of boyfriends, goes off to college and falls for her roommate. Her girl roommate.

I ride home, dazed, and just sit in the living room, thinking. When Mom and Dad get home, I look at them. I wonder if they know.

I look at them, at their tired faces, their sad eyes, and no, I don't think they do. I didn't know, and I saw more of the true Tess—her sweetness and the dark underneath it—than Mom and Dad ever did.

Should I tell them?

No. It isn't my story to tell. It was Tess's, and if she'd wanted to share it, she would have. But she kept it to herself.

We all have our own untold stories, and maybe this is what I can give Tess. I can let her keep her story, the hidden part of her heart, close to herself.

I just—I hope it is still with her. I hope that the self she knows is still somewhere inside her. I hope she . . .

I hope that deep inside, in the places none of us have been able to reach, that Tess is still there.

thirty-five

Now that I know about Beth, having Eli talk to Tess is—well, having him talk to her isn't necessary. But then, deep down, I know it hasn't really been about her, not like I wanted it to be since the first time I looked up from sitting with her and saw him looking at me.

Eli's waiting for me when I get to the hospital, sitting in the waiting room leaning intently over his notebook, pen in hand.

He looks up when I come in, though, like he knew I was coming. Like he's been waiting for me.

I tell myself to put a clamp on my brain. I know my heart isn't the problem. The heart is just a muscle and what makes it beat faster is the thoughts pounding in my head, Eli's name kick-thudding through me.

The brain clamp isn't really working, though, and I swear I feel it crack when he sees me and smiles. I force myself to think of Jack's face when he spoke about Tess, to remember how sure I was that I could make it change, that I could make that look mine. That I could make it about me.

The thing is, Eli's never once looked at Tess like Jack did.

The thing is, Eli's not Jack.

The thing is, I have no idea what to do. I haven't ever been wanted before, and even though part of me fears I'm seeing something that isn't there, an even bigger part of me fears that I am seeing something I never have before. That I am seeing something real—and for me.

"Hey," I say, before he can say anything. "I—this isn't—Tess's not getting any better. And I don't . . . I don't know if she ever will."

I didn't realize how true it would sound, how true I'm afraid it is, until I say it. For all the rage and fear that has driven me to the hospital day after day, something else has too. Hope.

I did believe Tess would wake up. I couldn't imagine a world without her fully in it. And trying to picture it now leaves me facing another truth I thought I'd grasped but really hadn't.

I love Tess. I want better for her than this. I want her to come back, to be here, to be whole.

"I'm sorry," Eli says, and I have heard those words like rain for months, over and over again, but they are new now. Eli is looking at me, and I see that he means he is sorry for me. For how I feel. He has always been able to cut through the words I push out, but it's more than that.

He sees me.

I'm going to tell him he doesn't have to meet me anymore. I'm going to say thank you if my lips can remember how to form those words. I'm going to . . .

"I'm going to go see her," I say. "Do you—do you want to come with me?"

I am—I have—said what I want to. For someone who is so good at snarling people away, I sure suck at it now.

But then, I don't want Eli to go. I wish I was better at lying to myself, but that wish vanishes as he smiles and says, "Yeah, of course," like there was never a question at all.

We pass Clement as we're walking to Tess's unit. He waves at us and says, "Abby, maybe I'll see you soon?"

"Like, right now?" I say, and he laughs his wheezy laugh and heads down the hall.

"He really likes you, you know," Eli says. "Told me I should invite you over to the house again."

"What, he has more ham he wants to unload?" I say as lightly as I can, simple words to replace the ones I want to say. The question I want to ask.

Do you want to see me again?

"Probably, but I promise I'll throw out all the ham if you're willing to come over for dinner one night," Eli says, his voice so quiet, so unsure, that I stop and look at him.

I can't talk; I have no words to shield myself with now. I don't want to shield myself. I nod. Yes, I will come over, yes, I am willing. *Yes.*

He grins at me then, so wide and lovely I actually feel lightheaded.

I wonder how many people Tess did that to with her smile.

If Beth once felt like I do now, caught and glad to be.

"What is it?" Eli says, and I can't believe how well he sees me. It makes me happy and scared and—it makes me feel a million things at once.

"Tess," I say. "I was just thinking about her because she—she had this way of smiling, you know? Like it was all you could see." I hear myself say "had" and want to change it, want to make it "has." But I can't. I know the truth now, have to face what I haven't wanted to see.

I turn away and start walking down the hall again. I feel myself relax when I hear Eli's footsteps behind me.

I let myself be glad he's with me.

"So, how come you call Clement, well—Clement?" I ask as we're waiting for the nurses to let us in.

"He says my dad called him Dad and acted like he didn't know him, so we could either pretend to be 'family' and I could call him Grandfather or something, or we could try being one, or even just try being two people who like each other enough to be more than a title," Eli says.

"He's kind of upset with your dad, I guess."

"No, sad," Eli says. "Not that he'd ever say it, I don't think, but it's hard to know that someone who's supposed to love you doesn't even want to see you."

I reach out, let my hand brush against Eli's. He turns his hand so our fingers tangle together, comfort without words as the buzzer sounds and we walk through the doors.

I watch the nurses take us in, our clasped hands, watch them turn toward each other, and then I pause by Tess's door, look inside her room. Look at her.

So still, so quiet. So alone.

"I have to tell you something," I say quietly, and I don't know if I'm talking to her or Eli or both of them.

And then I drop Eli's hand and walk into Tess's room, sit in the chair I always sit in. I turn it so it's a little closer to her bed. To her.

I look up, over to where Eli has sat, and he's there, looking at me.

"Tess," I say, looking back at her and thinking about Beth, about her touching Tess's hair, about her face when I asked her how she could act like Tess wasn't coming back. About those boxes, sitting lonely on the front lawn. "Tess, I—"

I don't tell her that I know her story. I tell her mine instead.

I tell her about Jack. I say all the things I didn't that summer, forgetting everything, even Eli, as the words pour out of me, right down to how loud the river sounded when I sat there after Jack said he was sorry, so sorry, and left.

"And the worst part was, I couldn't hate him," I tell her. "I couldn't hate you, even. I just . . . I thought I'd found someone who wanted to be with me. Kiss me. But I wouldn't let myself see what was obvious. I'm not you. I'm never going to be you."

She doesn't move. Doesn't blink. Doesn't do anything.

But Eli does. Eli gets out of his chair—I hear the sound of it moving back as he stands, and I look up, surprised, and see him walking toward me—and then he is there, kneeling right in front of me, and all the certainty I felt before is gone. He is too beautiful for me, someone else will see that and worse, see that inside he is gorgeous too, and I am all thorns and loss and anger with bony knees and then—

And then he kisses me.

thirty-six

"Why?" I say when I can breathe again, when I can think again, when we have separated because a nurse walked by and cleared her throat and I unwound my arms from around his neck and felt his leave the sides of my legs slowly, like he wanted to keep touching me. Keep kissing me.

He blinks at me like I'm speaking another language.

"Why?" I say again, and move so there is space between us, my gaze falling on Tess, a silent, unseeing witness to what has just happened.

"Because I—I'm someone who wants to kiss you. Be with you," Eli says as if it is obvious, as if I know what is written on his heart.

I look at him, still kneeling in front of me like I'm worthy of that. Like I'm worthy of what he just said. Like I'm worthy of him.

"Oh," I say, because I can't think of anything else to say, I can't find any words, not now, not after his, and look at him.

He is looking at me.

He is looking at me like everyone has always looked at Tess. As if I am someone worth seeing.

It's everything I've wanted, right down to Tess seeing it. But I never wanted Tess to see it like this. I never wanted her to be a silent, blind witness. I never wanted her here but gone, at least not like this. Never like this.

"Abby?" Eli says, his voice tentative, questions laced through each letter, and I know what comes next. It's easy. I take his hand, I say his name, and we will be together. But I don't . . .

I don't know if I'm ready for this. For him. I've spent so long wanting someone to see me—really see me—that I never thought about how it would feel if it happened.

It's not scary. It's past that, beyond that, and I don't know what to do now that this thing—this dream, and yes, that's what it's always been, a dream, an impossibility that came true only when my eyes were closed—is real.

It's not that I don't believe in the kiss or what he just said.

It's that I do. I believe he likes me, that he . . . that he sees me and wants me.

I don't know what to do with the happiness I feel, with the want racing through me. I have lived with broken need and anger and fear. I have lived with an ache to get out of Ferrisville, to get away. I have built worlds where I leave this place and become someone others want to see.

I've never pictured anyone finding me here. Wanting me here. I've never, ever pictured anyone like Eli.

"I don't know what to do," I say, and he'll know what to do, he has to know, this is the part where it will all work out. I haven't run away; I have stayed despite my fear and now this is real. Now we are real.

"Oh," he says, and I watch him move back, hands clenched in on themselves until he's back in his chair, where they rest on the arms and start to tap. "I thought—"

He shakes his head. His eyes aren't meeting mine now, and I don't understand. I haven't left. I haven't run. Why has he moved away? What's happening?

"You thought what?" I say, my heart pounding *please, please.*

His fingers are moving very fast now, and he stands up, a jerky, quick movement. "I should go," he says. "Let you think. Be with Tess."

"Eli—" I say, but he walks away. Going, going.

Gone.

I sit there, and this—being alone, having watched someone leave—it's more like what I'm used to. What I expect. But it feels wrong, and I am up and out of my chair suddenly, racing after him.

Tell me, I will say to him. *Tell me what you were going to say.*

But he's gone, and I can't find him anywhere. Even Clement is gone, the basement storage room that is now his office shut and locked.

So maybe Eli didn't mean what he said after all. I know all about that. I know what to do when a guy tries but can't quite make himself care for me.

I know what it's like to watch a guy walk away, but something is different now. I think of how Eli didn't look at me before he left. I think of all the questions I couldn't and don't understand that were in his voice when he said my name.

I could go to his house. Talk to Clement. Talk to him. There is no need to create drama here, I have enough in my life already, and I don't need to imagine how things will be when I'm away from Ferrisville anymore. Not now, not when I have said everything that was in my heart and Eli still wanted to look at me.

But it didn't go like it was supposed to. If it's real, if I saw what was in his heart, then why did he leave? Why am I here now, alone?

"What are you doing standing out here?" Claire says, and I jump, startled, and turn around, see her behind me.

"Hey," I say.

"Hey. What's going on?"

"Just . . ."

"Just what?"

"Nothing," I say, because I don't want to talk about it, not even with her. I want to understand what happened. I want to know how I took a moment that was so right and turned it wrong and why—worst of all—part of me is okay with that.

"You want a ride to the ferry?"

I shrug and she helps me load my bike into her car. I don't ask her to take me by Eli's. I don't even mention him.

I want to know why it is easier for me to stay quiet and be miserable than act. I want to know why I went after him, but only after he was gone. I want to know why I'm here, with Claire, instead of him.

"So, are you and Eli fighting or something?" Claire says as we are waiting for the ferry, and I fold my fingers up tight and sink down into the seat.

"Hey," she says, when I don't say anything. "Abby, are you—?"

"I'm fine."

"Bullshit," she says. "What happened?"

I force myself to talk because it's Claire and I trust her, and I don't finish the story until we are on the ferry and the river is churning beneath us.

When I do, I look over at her.

To my surprise, she's looking at me like I'm the dumbest person she's ever met.

"What?" I say.

"'I don't know what to do?'" she says. "What a load of crap, Abby. You tell him you want someone to want to be with you, to kiss you—and he says that, he actually fucking kisses you and says that, and you say you don't know what to do and then wonder why he left? How stupid are you?"

"I'm not—"

"Yeah, you're not stupid," she says. "You're just like your sister, though. You're so sure things have to be a certain way that you'll do anything to make sure they are. God forbid you be honest with yourself and him, right? God forbid you say 'I want to kiss you too.'"

"I figured that was implied by me kissing him back. I mean—"

"Oh, sure, because there's nothing like putting your heart out there and getting nothing in return to make a girl feel good," she says, so angry she's practically spitting. "You're sitting here feeling sorry for yourself when all you had to do was be honest with him and—"

"I was honest."

"No, you weren't. You know what you want. You know what to do. You're just afraid. I didn't realize exactly how much you're like—you and fucking Tess, I swear."

"I'm not like—"

"You're *exactly* like her," Claire says. "You want to be loved but when you are, if it's not exactly how you expected it to be—if it's real and you have to deal with feelings you can't control, you freak out and push the other person away and—" She takes a deep breath. "Get out of my car."

"What?"

"You heard me," she says. "Get out of my car."

"But I—"

"I swear to God, if you don't get out I will push you out," she says, and I stare at her furious face, so like Tess's the day she found out Claire was pregnant, so much like Tess's the day Claire walked by the house and Tess ran outside to throw food at her, furious like—

Furious like her heart had been broken.

"Tess," I breathe, stunned, and Claire freezes.

thirty-seven

"Get out," she says, but there's no heat in her voice now. No anger. Only pleading.

I stare at her. "Tess was . . . you and Tess?"

Claire is silent for a long moment and then nods once, slowly.

"And then you . . . you got pregnant and—"

"I had Cole," Claire says, her voice going hard again. "And now here I am."

"So when Tess found out, she wasn't mad you were pregnant—"

"She wasn't?" Claire says, cutting me off. "She made it so I had to drop out of school, Abby. You don't call that angry?"

I think of how sorry I used to feel for Claire. How I used to think that Tess was cruel for turning away from her best friend because she got pregnant like it was a crime or something.

Like she couldn't bear to be around Claire anymore.

"You . . . you broke her heart," I say. "You knew how she felt and you hooked up with Rick and—"

"Abby—"

"No," I say, and keep talking. "That's why you never said much of anything about Beth, right? Why you always smiled when I talked about them living together. You knew, and you'd hurt her, and I thought she was being cruel when you—"

"Stop," Claire says, and I realize we are moving, that the ferry has docked and Claire is driving off the boat. Driving back into Ferrisville. "You don't—Tess dated guys too, Abby."

"Yeah," I say slowly, thinking of all the guys who'd called Tess, who'd hung around her. How she'd talk to them, maybe see them at a party or go on one date, maybe two, and then send them on their way. None of them had turned her into the furious, hate-filled person that Claire had.

None of them had ever touched her heart.

"But not like you did," I say, and she recoils like I've hit her, then pulls over to the side of the road.

"I—I can't do this right now," she says. "I have to go home."

"You mean, I've figured out what really happened and you don't want to talk about it," I say, my voice harsh. "You don't want to think about how you broke Tess's heart, right?"

"Abby, come on. I have to see Cole and I can't—I don't want him to see me upset."

"She told you, right? She told you how she felt and you—you got mad at her or something and—"

Claire laughs, harsh and angry. "That's your story, Abby? She told me she loved me, and I ran out and got pregnant so she'd stay away from me. Is that how it went?"

"I didn't say—"

"Yeah, because I stopped you," Claire says. "We both know you were thinking it. And you know what, Abby? Even Tess wouldn't think something like that. Even Tess knew—" She blows out a breath. "Even Tess knew me better than that. I thought you weren't like her, that you didn't have some fucked-up version of the world and your place in it in your head, but you know what? You do."

"I blamed Tess!" I yell. "You hurt her, and I thought Tess was stupid and mean and I—I felt sorry for you!"

"It's not like you—" Claire says, and then breaks off as someone driving by slows down long enough to wave at us and then make a gesture asking if we're okay.

"I can't do this," she says again. "I have to get home to Cole."

"Fine," I say, and open the car door and grab my bike. "But at least tell me why, okay? Why did you hurt her when she just— she just loved you."

Claire stares at me for a moment, like she's lost, and then she says, "Why are you so sure I hurt her?"

"So you getting pregnant and making Tess miserable had nothing to do with Tess?"

Claire looks at the steering wheel for a long time before she speaks, and when she does, her voice is so quiet I can barely hear her. "It had everything to do with her. I . . . she only ever said she loved me, Abby."

I slam the door shut and walk off.

Tess told Claire she loved her. That was it, and when she said it, Claire freaked out, and all those times I felt bad for her, Tess was the one who was hurting, Tess was the one who'd put her heart out there and gotten it stomped on.

If I'd known, I'd—

If I'd known, Tess and I—we could have talked. I thought nothing reached her, that nobody had ever held her heart, that she'd judged Claire for not acting like she would have, but all this time—

All this time, I could have had my sister.

thirty-eight

I get home—I didn't look at Claire's house when
I went by, I won't ever look at it the same now—and stand in the
kitchen in a daze, thinking about all the times Tess railed against
Claire during her last year of high school, and finally see her anger
for what it was.

Pain.

I walk up to Tess's room, glad I am alone now, glad my parents are with Tess, that she has someone with her who loves her
without all the complications I've been carrying around.

I wish I'd never thought anything bad about her.

I look around her room, at the boxes on the floor. I think
about what's inside them. Her life with Beth and now it's here,

wrapped up and in the middle of the floor, just sitting here waiting.

I wonder if Beth knew about Claire.

Poor Tess. She's lost two people she loved. I've always thought she got everything—everyone—she wanted.

I was so wrong.

I sit down at her desk, run my fingers across her laptop. Now I understand why Tess never looked at Claire, not even whenever she'd come home from college. Not even after she'd met Beth. I thought she was still angry. I thought she was being petty.

Tess was angry, but I can see why now, and I'll bet she was sad too. And hurt, hurt enough to avoid Claire for years. To still think about what had happened. What Claire did, how Tess loved her and Claire . . . didn't. Not like Tess loved her.

My fingers slide across the laptop's power button, and when the screen lights up, asking me for the password, I don't think at all. I type *Claire*, and the welcome screen appears.

I stare at it. All this time, and the password was right in front of me. All this time and Tess—her real story, who she really was—was right in front of me.

And I never saw it.

I take a look around her computer, checking out her files. I should feel guilty, but I don't. I want to know the real Tess, the sister I never met, but there isn't much to see. I find some papers Tess wrote, some music she downloaded, and a folder labeled "photos" that has pictures of her and Beth. No guys in them, no pretense.

I can see they are a couple in these photos, see them with

their arms around each other, Tess smiling broader and with more joy than I've ever seen. I think about the photos she brought home for us to see, and how she laughed whenever I asked about the guys in them.

These photos, the ones with Beth, hold the real Tess, and I decide I'll copy and transfer them to my computer. Then I'll print one out and take it with me when I see Tess again tomorrow. I want to—I want to let Tess know I see her for who she really is, and not who I made her out to be.

But when I try to select the files, I get a message that there are two hidden ones.

Hidden files?

I open the menu that controls file viewing options and make all files and folders visible. Two more folders pop up on screen within the "photos" folder I'm looking at. One is labeled "beth messages," and the other "over."

I can guess what the "over" folder is about, think of Beth telling me Tess had decided they shouldn't live together anymore.

I click on it anyway, expecting something that will tell me what went wrong. That will show me how Tess lost something—someone—I never even knew was in her heart.

But it's not what I see.

thirty-nine

There are pictures and online message conversations in the folder, jumbled together as if Tess had copied
them from somewhere else in a hurry. Like she had to have
them but hadn't wanted to see them, not even to organize them
in any way.

I click on one of the saved messages, and a huge, pages-long
conversation opens.

It's not . . . it's not from Tess's time in college. It's from
when she was in high school. I can tell because she's talking about
teachers I have now.

At the end of the message, Claire—and I know it's her,
because I know her screen name, like I know Tess's, like I used to

know everything about them, or thought I did—has typed:

sigh. dinner time find u later xo always

I look for Tess's reply but there isn't one. Just that last line, from Claire. *xo always*

I don't—what is this?

I close the message and click on one of the photos. It's of Tess, and was taken before she was a senior. I can tell from her hair, which is long, practically down to her waist. She only wore it short her last year in high school, cut it so it barely reached her shoulders right after—

Right after she found out about Claire.

In the picture, Tess and Claire are lying on Tess's bed, grinning up at the camera and snuggled against each other like . . . like friends, but more. You can see it in how one of Tess's hands rests on Claire's leg, lies curved familiar above her knee.

You can see it in how Claire is turned toward Tess, one hand tangled in Tess's hair as the other holds the camera above them. Both of them are smiling, and they look . . .

They look happy.

They look like they're together.

I click through a few more photos. Some of them are like the one I just saw, and some of them make everything even clearer, show Claire's bare back shielding Tess's front as Tess grins up at the camera she's holding, eyes half closed.

In the last one I look at, Tess's head is resting in the crook of Claire's neck as her hands cover Claire's breasts, and Claire has her eyes closed, her mouth turned toward Tess, seeking.

I have to sit and look at the floor for a little bit after that one. I just . . . Tess and Claire. All those times they were in here with the door closed, listening to music and working on homework, they were . . .

No wonder Tess always yelled at me for trying to come in her room without knocking.

I look at the dates on the photos, and they seem to run from Tess and Claire's freshman year to right after their senior year started. To right before Tess came home and spit out, "Claire's pregnant."

The last two photos are dated about the time I figure Claire got pregnant. The first one is in Claire's room—I've seen Cole scrabbling across the comforter that lies tangled on the bed.

It's morning, and Tess is lying on her stomach, sleeping, her closed eyes facing the camera but not seeing it. Not seeing anything. The light is tangled in her hair, shining off it and the bare skin of her back. She looks otherworldly, beautiful.

Underneath, someone has added *Bliss* in an elegant, cursive font, like they tried to title the photo.

The second photo shows Tess at a party on the beach, sitting and talking to a guy. She's smiling, mouth curved wide, familiar, but her eyes are looking at the camera, not him, and they look—

They look sad, but they look angry too.

The same font has been used to label this photo as well. It says *Your Choice*.

I stare at it, wondering who wrote those words—Tess? Claire?—and what they mean. I know what happened, but there's something . . . there's something I'm not getting. Not seeing.

I close the folder and open the other one, "beth messages." There's only one thing in it, and it was last opened—

It was last opened on New Year's Eve, right before Tess left for her party.

It's another online conversation, but it's not from that night. It's from before, from Tess's last semester in school, from last fall, and from the first line, when someone says, *I need to talk to u,* I know it's a fight.

I think it must be the fight that ended things.

It's hard to tell, though, because the person I think is Beth (Beth0728—it has to be her) is the only one talking.

She says she needs Tess to trust her, and that she wants to stop pretending.

There's no reply, but Beth keeps writing, types that she knows who she is, and adds that *everyone knows about us already.*

Still no reply, and Beth types, *i don't know why you cant admit it. i want us to be together for real i want to be able to say this is my girlfriend.*

Still no reply and Beth types, *say something say anything don't get all quiet on me okay? Please? Tess?*

Nothing and Beth types, *fine. i can't take it anymore. you have to do this or it's over. OVER. you know Im not Claire I won't break your heart.*

Tess finally types something back then.

She types, *I broke my own heart.*

"Oh," I say, and my voice is loud in the silent room, so loud

I can hear it above the roaring in my ears, hear it past the words I've just read and the memory of those photos of Claire and Tess.

Claire and Tess and in the very last photo, Claire wasn't in it at all. It was just Tess and that guy, Tess smiling at him as she stared at the camera. Stared at whoever was taking the picture like she was sad and angry. Stared, but wasn't moving. Was sitting by the guy's side like it was where she wanted to be. Had to be.

Claire took the photo. Claire was the one Tess was looking at.

Your Choice.

Claire told me, "She only ever *said* she loved me," and now I realize what that means. What Tess did. She said it, but only in private. She said it, but would never, ever do anything more. Anything public.

Claire didn't break Tess's heart. Tess broke hers.

I just don't know why. Was it because Claire got pregnant? Did Claire cheat on her and Tess couldn't—wouldn't—forgive her?

I broke my own heart.

Those words are so familiar. Too familiar.

I call Beth, because she'll know what happened. She has to, but as soon as I say, "It's Abby, Tess's sister," she says, "I'm not talking to you. I know you're angry, but you have to understand that I can't—"

"But that's just it," I say. "I didn't understand, but now I do, and I just want to know why you and Tess broke up."

Beth laughs and it sounds so much like Claire's laugh when she talked about Tess before, so brittle and angry and sad, that my skin prickles.

"*Why?*" she says. "You want to know why, like it's just one reason, just one thing?"

"Okay, I'm sure it was complicated, and I didn't mean—I just want to know what happened. You lived with her, you two were—"

"I can't talk about this," Beth says. "I just—I can't."

"You mean you won't."

"No," Beth says. "I mean I can't. I don't know why she wouldn't admit we were together. Go ask Claire, always lurking around her hospital room, always hanging around in Tess's head, always—always there."

"Claire?"

"What, you're surprised? You didn't know?"

"I do, but I don't exactly know what happened."

"I don't either," Beth says, her voice weary. "All I ever knew is that something happened with Tess and Claire and—well, my guess is Tess freaked out because Claire ran off and had a baby rather than admit she loved Tess and it fucked Tess up. Ask Claire if you want to know. It's not like—God, it's not like you haven't had the chance."

"But—"

"No," Beth says. "Two years, okay? I loved Tess so much and she loved me but not enough, never enough, and I finally told her to choose and she just—she shut down, spent the rest of the semester looking through me, and now she's in the hospital and I won't ever—" She sniffs once, twice, like she's struggling not to cry. "I've had to let her go and I can't—don't call here again."

And then she hangs up.

"What are you doing?"

I look over my shoulder and see Mom standing in Tess's doorway, glancing from the computer to the phone in my hand, and then to me. She looks worried but not surprised, and I wonder if she's trying to figure out why I'm in Tess's room.

"I was—" I point at Tess's computer. "I was just looking for something. A file. For school."

"On Tess's computer?" Mom says, shaking her head at my transparent lie, and I say, "I just—Tess was—is—" and watch her expression change ever so slightly.

Watch her realize I've found out something she already knows.

Mom knows, and I stand up, putting the phone down as I say, "You . . . why didn't you tell me about Tess?"

I figure Mom will try to talk her way out of it, say she wanted to wait or something like that. But she doesn't.

She just says, "It wasn't my place to tell."

"Wasn't your place?" I can hear my voice rising. "All this time I thought Tess—"

"What?" Mom says, eyes narrowing, and I think she actually believes I'm going to judge Tess for who she cared about, that I—

"Hey!" I say. "I'm not—you mean you didn't tell me because you thought I'd, what? Try to set her on fire? What kind of person do you think I am?"

"Abby," she says, coming toward me and touching my arm. "I didn't—"

"You did too."

"No," she says softly. "I didn't. I don't. I—I just don't know what you know."

"How about Tess was in love with Claire, and I'm pretty sure Claire loved her, but it looks like Tess got hurt. And then she met Beth but couldn't bring herself to admit they were a couple, so—"

"We'd better go downstairs and talk," Mom says. "There's . . . there's some things your father and I need to tell you."

"You mean there's more?" I say, stunned, and Mom nods before turning away. I hear her walking downstairs.

After a moment, I follow.

forty

I figure we'll sit in the living room stiffly, like we're strangers, and that Mom and Dad will be nervous, look at each other as they tell me about Tess, using each other's expressions to figure out what to say and how to say it.

Instead, we sit in the kitchen and eat dinner like we used to. Like we did when Tess was home. Like we did before her accident, back when Mom and Dad wondered out loud about how Tess was doing, gesturing at her empty chair like she was still there as they talked about their days and asked me about mine.

I'm not prepared for this, for how easily my parents start talking about Tess, Dad glancing at Mom as I sit down and nodding once before saying, "I don't know if Tess would have ever told us anything if I hadn't walked in on her and Claire when I went to tell them good night back when they were fifteen."

"You might not remember," Mom says, passing me a bowl of corn. "You were twelve, and—"

"The night Claire went home because she was sick from eating too much ice cream, only I never saw her eat any, right?" I say, and Mom nods.

I always knew something had happened then. I just didn't know what.

"Anyway, we sent Claire home because—well." She clears her throat.

"You were surprised," I say, still feeling pretty surprised myself, especially as I watch Dad take the smallest amount of corn he can, just like he always does. Shouldn't there be drama? Shouldn't we at least be speaking in hushed voices or something? Shouldn't it not be so . . . normal?

"Well, yes," Dad says. "We were surprised. But Tess—well, she was the one who asked Claire to go."

"Dave," Mom says, fondness and exasperation lacing her voice, and gives him another scoop of corn before looking at me. "So then your father and I talked to Tess. And yes, before you ask, that's why we let you stay up late and watch television downstairs."

"Right," I say, watching as Dad sneaks the extra corn back into the bowl just like he always . . . just like he always did back when us eating dinner like this was normal.

But this isn't normal.

We haven't eaten dinner together in ages, not like this, so

why now? Why tonight? They didn't know I knew about Tess, there's no way they could have, so this dinner—

They planned it. Before Mom found me in Tess's room, this was going to happen. They set this up to tell me something, I'm sure of it.

But what?

"What's going on?" I ask, my voice sharp, and Mom glances at Dad, and Dad glances back at her like I thought they would at first, like how I'd pictured. Like they're trying to figure out what to say. How to say it.

"Just tell me," I snap when neither of them speaks, and Mom looks at me as if she's never seen me before.

As she does, I realize there is a lot she doesn't know about me. I've kept myself hidden from her and Dad just like Tess kept herself hidden from me.

"First of all, don't talk to your mother like that," Dad says. "And second—" He picks up a piece of chicken like he's going to take a bite, like this is still a real dinner, like Tess is going to walk through the door. Like she's still really here.

"Stop it," I hiss. "Stop pretending, stop—just stop all of this and tell. me. what's. going. on."

Dad frowns, clearly unhappy with my tone, but Mom leans over and squeezes his hand. "We spoke to the hospital today," she says. "We've made arrangements for Tess. The day after tomorrow, we're having her moved and we—we'd like you to be there, Abby."

I crack into a million pieces then. How can I not, with Eli and Claire and Tess—who she was, who she is—how can I not crack when I have all these unknowns? How can I not crack when Tess's being taken out of the hospital? When she's being written off?

How can I stay whole when everything has changed so much, so fast?

"I—you're really doing it? You're willing to say this is it, this is the rest of her life, forever lying in a bed somewhere not seeing the world, not seeing anything?"

"Abby, honey, we're only moving her," Mom says at the same time Dad says, "Abby, it's not like—you know it's not like that. Tess could wake up, she could. But we—"

He breaks off then, and looks at Mom.

"We're moving her," he finally says, his voice very soft. "We have to. She's just—" He clears his throat. "She's just not ready to come back. At least not now."

I can't believe this is happening. Why now, when I see that I've been so wrong about Tess, that I don't even know her at all? I mean, her whole life; all the plans and excitement about seeing guys, about talking to them, all of that—all of them—meant nothing to her, but Claire—Claire meant everything. Tess and Claire were together, and Dad found out and Tess asked Claire to . . .

Wait.

"Hold on. You said Tess told Claire to leave when you—when you found them?" I ask Dad, and just like that dinner collapses. Oh, we're still here and the food is still here, but nobody's eating now, and the tension I was sure would be here before is out now, smothering the room in silence.

It stays like that, so quiet—too quiet—for a long time, and then Mom puts her fork down, pretense done.

"Tess didn't—she said she wasn't . . ." And my mother—my always together, always polished mother—gestures at the air helplessly, like the words she's looking for are just out of reach.

"She said she wasn't a lesbian," Dad says, and when Mom looks at him, he says, "We have to tell her everything, Katie."

"Tell me everything?" What else could there be?

Dad pushes his plate away. "Your sister wasn't—she wasn't comfortable talking about her sexuality."

Well, there's a word I don't ever want to hear Dad say again. He must somehow know I'm thinking it too, because he gives me a small, sad half smile and says, "Tess looked at me like you just did whenever I tried to talk to her. Said she and Claire were friends, and the way I understood the world had changed."

"But—"

"But they were more than friends," Mom said. "We could see that. Tess and Claire spent so much time together, and neither of them ever dated anyone else, not seriously, but Tess would never talk to us, never—"

"Never admit it?" I say, and Mom shakes her head.

"It's not that simple, Abby. She eventually told me she did have feelings for Claire but that she—she was afraid."

"Afraid?" I say, and then think about Claire. About Cole. "Oh. She was afraid Claire didn't—?"

"I don't know—no, that's not true," Mom says, and folds her hands together. "I don't think she was afraid that Claire didn't care about her too. She knew that she did. I think Tess was afraid that if she—"

"Came out?"

"No," Dad says, touching Mom's hands briefly. "She was afraid that if she admitted she loved Claire, she would lose her. Your sister was—she had some problems."

"Like being afraid to come out?"

Dad shakes his head, and Mom knots her hands together so tightly her knuckles go stark white, bloodless. When she speaks, she sounds like she's trying not to cry. "She . . . Tess was a lot like my mother. Even as a child she could be so happy one minute, and then the next she'd pull away from the world."

She looks at Dad, who nods at her, and Mom closes her eyes. When she opens them, they are wet with unshed tears. "Do you remember when Tess went to see the college admissions counselor during her senior year?"

I shrug, but I remember. How could I not? She pitched such a fit about everything, and my parents wanted to help her get into the school she wanted to go to, wanted to—

Wanted to help her.

"Oh," I say. "So senior year, she wasn't—all those times she went to talk about getting into college, she wasn't talking about college at all, was she?"

"You must have noticed how she acted after Claire got pregnant," Dad says. "She was—"

"Upset," I say, and think of how Tess's sometimes moodiness had come more often and gotten stronger, worse. All those things she did—like the meatballs, that sudden furious, frightening outburst—and I never thought—

"I didn't know," I say. "I thought . . . She was Tess. She always—everyone said she was so amazing. So perfect."

"She wasn't," Dad says. "She was . . . she was very unhappy."

"But she got better," I say. "Right? She went to school and met Beth and—" I pause, look at Mom and Dad. "Did she ever tell you that she and Beth were together?"

"No," Mom says. "We'd hoped she would, but I guess after Claire she was—I think maybe she was afraid she'd get her heart broken again."

I broke my own heart.

I swallow.

"So, what exactly happened with Claire?"

"We don't know," Dad says. "We knew they were seeing each other, but how it ended—we assume it's because Claire got pregnant, but we didn't even know about that until Tess told us. Do you remember when she did that?"

As if I could forget that day, Tess coming home and going straight up to her room, not even taking phone calls, and when Mom asked how Claire was at dinner, Tess had stared at her for what felt like forever before she finally said, "Pregnant," spitting the word out like it was poison. After that, she'd left the room whenever anyone said Claire's name.

I look at Mom and Dad, so close, so together, and think of the last two photos of Claire and Tess. The first one, Tess lit up like an angel, sleeping in Claire's bed as if she belonged there. The second, Tess staring at the camera and smiling even though her eyes were so not happy.

Your Choice.

"I have to go," I tell them, standing up, and they both rise too, questions in their eyes.

"I have to get out of here, I have to think," I say. "Today has been . . . I thought I knew Tess, but I—was she ever who I thought she was? Is anyone who they say they are?"

They don't answer me.

They don't have to. Tess wasn't who I thought she was, and you can never fully know anyone, not ever.

I see that now. I see so much now.

I leave the house and start walking down the street.

Claire is sitting on her porch, staring up into the sky, and I stop at the end of her driveway, wait for her to look down. Look away from whatever she's watching—or thinking about—and see me.

forty-one

Claire doesn't look at me, though. She's staring up at the sky like she's reading it, like the stars are speaking to her, and so I clear my throat and say, "Hey."

She looks away from the sky then, looks at me. It's hard to see her face from where I stand because she's sitting so the porch light cuts her into areas of light and dark, shadowing her eyes but showing the fingers of one hand curled up tight.

"You want to talk about Tess," she says, and there's no question in her voice at all.

"I found—" I say, and then stop, thinking of the photos. Of Claire's face turned toward Tess's, of the two of them smiling. Of the picture Claire took of Tess sleeping. Of how Tess had them all hidden, like she wanted to pretend they never were.

I bet that's what Claire wants too.

"I found out," I say. "I figured it out."

Claire moves into the light then, motions for me to sit on the porch with her. "Just—be quiet, okay? Cole's asleep and you know how he wakes up super easily."

"I know."

"I know you know," she says, and then sighs. "How did you figure it out?"

"Well, you were—there was everything you said in the car, you know," I say. "And then I went home and started thinking. And then I walked by Tess's room and remembered how, um—"

"You found something," Claire says, and for the first time, she sounds surprised. "Tess kept—she kept things?"

"Pictures," I mutter. "On her computer."

"Oh," Claire says. "So you know know."

"Yeah. Or at least, I think I do."

"If you saw what I think you did, I don't see how you can not know," Claire says. "Wait, did that make any sense?"

"No," I say, and she grins at me.

"I didn't—if I'd known we'd be friends I wouldn't have—"

"Kept it from me?"

"Ever talked to you," she says. "I don't—"

She takes a deep breath.

"I wanted Tess to go away and never come back. I wanted her to—I wanted her to tell me she was wrong. That she was sorry."

"I'm sure she is," I say, though I'm not really sure at all. How can I be, when the Tess I knew never spoke Claire's name, but the

Tess I didn't kept pictures and remembered her every time she used her computer?

"No," Claire says. "She isn't. She—I had to drop out of school because of her, Abby. She made my life hell."

"Well," I say slowly because she's right, Tess did ruin high school for Claire. "I guess she—I guess she was so hurt when you got pregnant that she felt like she'd broken her own heart for thinking you wanted her like she wanted you, and—"

"What?" Claire says, and the word is so sharp and loud that down the street, a dog barks, and inside Claire's house, Cole stirs, calling, "Mommy?"

Claire gets up and goes inside. I can't hear what she says to Cole but I hear the sound of her voice, a faint, calm thread. Eventually, it fades into silence.

I sit on the porch, waiting until I start to think Claire isn't coming back out. She finally does, though, a pack of cigarettes in one hand, a lighter in the other.

"I thought you were quitting," I say, and she says, "I thought you wouldn't still be here," and sits back down next to me.

"I don't know the whole story," I say.

"Are you sure you want to?"

I nod and Claire pulls out a cigarette and lights it. Its scent rises up to me, harsh and with a chemical tinge that reminds me, weirdly, of the hospital. I wave the smoke away.

"It's funny, but I didn't start smoking until I got the job at the hospital," Claire says. "I was so excited back then. Finally, I had my GED, I had a job, I could take care of me and Cole—well, at least take care of us if we lived at home. But that place, it just—"

She looks at me. "There's no good way to die, you know? No way I've seen, anyway. It all ends with tubes and bedpans and IVs and I just—smoking gets me out of there. Gets me outside, gets me away from all the—"

"Sick people?" I say, and she shakes her head.

"Away from my life. This isn't—I wanted to go to college, Abby. I wanted . . ." She sighs. "I wanted Tess. But she—she didn't want me. Not like I wanted her."

"She must have, because I know you two—"

"Yeah, we had sex," Claire says. "And she even said she loved me. But she didn't—I asked her, right before senior year, to stop with the guys. To stop pretending. I mean, I know it's Ferrisville, but it's not like we'd have gotten lynched. Your parents already knew, and mine—well, what did I care then? I was going to get out of this place."

"Wait a minute," I say, thinking of the picture of Tess and the guy on the beach. Of the anger in Tess's eyes and how I assumed it was because Claire had hurt her, gone off with a guy like Tess had, only for real. "I thought—"

"You thought I got pregnant and broke Tess's heart."

"Yeah. I mean, before that, back when I thought you were just friends, I thought she was mad at you for—I don't know. I thought she was judging you. You know how Tess could be. She liked things to be—"

"How she wanted them," Claire says. "Believe me, I know."

"But you two weren't just friends, and she—"

"Tess couldn't do it," Claire says. "Wouldn't do it. Wouldn't stop being who everyone thought she was, even though it wasn't who she was. She said that if we—she said if we told everyone we were together, we wouldn't be who people thought we were. That's just how she said it too. 'If we do this, Claire, nobody will think we're who we say we are.'" She looks down at the ground.

I think she's going to cry so I say, "Claire?" and touch her shoulder.

She looks at me and I see she isn't going to cry. She's furious, so angry her mouth is working like it's full of words and she's trying to get them to come out in order.

"It was such a load of crap," she says. "Tess just—she wanted to be Homecoming Queen like everyone said she would be. She wanted everyone to keep trying to dress like her, be like her. She didn't want—she wanted to be *Tess*, the girl every guy wanted and dreamed about having even if he had a girlfriend. She didn't want to be Tess, the gay girl."

"Wait," I say, because this is not what I pictured, this is not what I pictured at all. I can see Tess being the one to break Claire's heart. I remember the pictures and can see them for what they are now, how Claire used them to show Tess what she'd felt they'd lost. What she thought Tess had given up. "My parents said Tess—they said she—"

Stupidly, absurdly, I lower my voice, as if someone might hear, as if what I'm going to say could be somehow overheard. As if Tess could somehow hear it now. "They said she had to go see a doctor. They said she was upset and—"

Claire shrugs. "Maybe she was. Maybe after she told me we had to be who people thought we were, and I said no when she wanted to mess around and then went off and screwed Rick and got pregnant, proved I could be straighter than she ever could—yeah, then maybe she might have gotten upset."

"No, I think she—I think my parents meant she was upset over you."

"Over me?" Her voice cracks on the last word. "She wasn't upset over me."

I think of Tess refusing to let any of us even say Claire's name. I think about the day with the meatballs. I think about how Tess always turned away whenever she saw Claire, or Claire and Cole, like she didn't want to see them. Like she couldn't.

"Look, I know how Tess is—was," I say, and it hurts to say that, to put Tess in the past tense. Even now, hearing that she broke Claire's heart because she wanted to keep on being the girl everyone wanted, the girl who was always just out of reach, it hurts.

I didn't know I loved Tess this much. Not until now.

I look down at the ground, blinking hard, my eyes burning.

"I know how she was," I say after a moment. "She was—she loved being adored, and I . . . you know I hated living with that. Being Tess's little sister. Being the one who wasn't as nice, who wasn't as pretty. Being the one who had to watch her get everything she wanted. But she—when she found out that you were pregnant, she changed. It was like she had . . . like she decided her life was a role or something. She'd go out smiling, but at home she was upset. She was so silent sometimes."

"Oh, so she was quiet?" Claire says, and although there's scorn in her voice I hear something else too, something wounded and hesitant, and think of how Claire always manages to come by Tess's room at the hospital.

I think love is huge, overwhelming. I think it's terrible and beautiful, and I wish Tess had found a way to live with it. To let it in when she had the chance. I wish she hadn't broken Claire and then broken herself.

"I never saw her cry," I say carefully. "But she . . . she would come home and sit in her room and just stare at nothing for hours, and I thought—well, my parents told me she was worried about college, and you know how her grades were."

"I remember," Claire says, but I can tell she is thinking of something else. Of a Tess I never knew at all.

"She was unhappy," I say. "She was—"

"And I was what, spinning around full of joy?" Claire says. "Tess broke my heart and then made life impossible for me. She was beyond cruel."

"Your name is her computer password," I say in a rush. "She kept pictures you sent her. She even—you're the reason why she and Beth broke up. She didn't—"

"What? Love Beth the way she loved me?" Claire says. "I've seen Beth visit her, I see how Beth looks at her. I know that look. Tess wouldn't choose her either. Beth was just smart enough to be the one who left."

"It's not—I don't think she knew how much . . ." I take a deep breath. "I don't think she knew how much she loved you until you got pregnant. Until you . . . I guess maybe she thought you'd come back or—"

"You know the really pathetic thing?" Claire says. "I would have. I would have gone back. I told her I wanted to actually kiss her in public, that I wanted people to see how much I loved her, but I would have kept on being the best friend. I would have kept on going on double dates with her and making out in my room, in the dark, when we got home."

She taps ash off her cigarette. "I would have done anything for her. But she couldn't get over the fact that I got drunk, had sex, and got pregnant. She couldn't understand it. That's what she said. 'I don't understand.' Sometimes I think that's what made her the maddest, you know. That I could want somebody else, even if it was for just a little while."

"Tess wasn't—she isn't evil, you know." I'm surprised to hear myself say it, because there have been times when I've pretty much hated Tess. Times before the accident. After the accident. But she wasn't—she wasn't who I thought she was. And now that I've learned more about her, the real her, I see what a mess she made of things. How imperfect she was.

How she could and did break her own heart too.

"I know," Claire says, and then seeing my face, adds, "I do. Now, anyway. The first time she came home from college and I saw her, I didn't feel like I was going to die. I just thought, 'Oh, there's Tess. I wonder if Cole's hungry.' Having him—" She shrugs. "I couldn't think about just me anymore. I can't think about just me anymore."

"But you miss her."

"No," Claire says, shaking her head. "I just—I look at her lying there, and I think, *No*. I think *Wrong*. I wish she'd wake up. I wish we were fifteen again. I wish I'd never met her. I wish she'd said, 'I want you, just you.' I wish she'd said she was sorry for everything."

233

"She would have . . ." I say, and then stop, because I don't know if Tess would have. The Tess I know wouldn't—she never apologized for anything because she never had to, because she never did anything wrong. But the other Tess, the real Tess, maybe she wouldn't have either. Maybe she knew some things are too big for "sorry."

Maybe she knew what she'd done to Claire couldn't be forgiven.

"Look, sometimes you just have to live with how things are, even if they aren't how you want them to be," Claire says.

"I want her to be sorry."

"I want her to be sorry too," Claire says, stubbing out her cigarette. "But I'd also like to be able to move out of my parents' house and meet someone who wants to hold my hand where people can see."

"You'll meet that someone," I say, and she looks at me.

"No," she says. "I probably won't. I'm twenty, with a two-year-old, and I live with my parents in a town where everyone is pretty much each other's cousin. I get up, I take a shower, I go to work. I give dying people sponge baths and change bedpans. I come home, I see my son, I go to bed."

"That doesn't mean you can't be happy."

"Who says I'm not happy?" Claire says, and then grins at me. "I'm not unhappy, Abby. I just am. I have Cole, I have my parents, I have a job. It's enough."

"It's not," I say, so strongly I surprise myself.

"Why not?" she says. "Look at you. You're doing the same thing. Before the accident, you got up, you went to school, you came home. Now you get up, you go to school, you see Tess, you come home. You totally blew off El—"

"I don't want to talk about Eli," I mutter. "Especially not if you're going to bitch at me again."

"Fine," Claire says. "Throw away something that could be great because you don't know what's going to happen. Go ahead and—"

"I'm not like Tess."

"Yeah, you are, because you're afraid too. Not of the same things she was, but you're still afraid. You know what I wish someone had told me back when I was trying to decide what to do after Tess said sorry, she wanted things to stay the way they were?"

"That you were better off without her?"

Claire shakes her head. "No, I told myself that. I told myself lots of stuff like that, right up until I woke up, went to take a shower, and realized I hadn't had my period in a while. I wish someone had told me to believe I deserved what I wanted, that wanting Tess to love me like I did her was okay. I wish someone had told me I deserved to be happy. I wish . . . I wish I'd believed I deserved to be."

"But that's so obvious," I say. "I mean, everyone knows they deserve some happiness. That's all people think life should be, Claire. Happily ever after all the time. It's not—no one wants to be unhappy."

"You do."

"I—yeah, I asked for Tess to be my sister. I asked for her to be in an accident. I asked to live here. I asked for all of it, when all along, I should have been asking for candy and ponies. What was I thinking?"

"You know I'm right," Claire says. "I can tell, because you've gotten all bitchy." She looks down at her hands, and then at me.

"Look," she says. "I'm going to say this to you because I really do wish someone had said it to me, even though right now you're being a total pain in the ass. But you—Abby, you can be happy. You should be. And I wish you would see that. I wish you would believe it."

There is so much sorrow in her voice, and it's not just for her, it's for me, and it breaks my heart.

It makes me think. "Claire—"

She stands up. "I'm going to bed."

"I'm sorry," I say.

"For Tess?"

"No. I mean, yes, for what she did, but also for not—I should have known you would never hurt her. You aren't that kind of person. And what you said, I just, you know . . ."

"You're welcome," Claire says, and then laughs a little. "Only in Ferrisville could my best friend be my former never-really-real-girlfriend's younger sister. Although I think you trying to say thank you is weirder."

"If I believe what you said, will you believe it too?"

"No," Claire says softly. "I won't. I can't. I'm not—I'm not strong enough to now. When Cole's older, and money isn't so tight, and I have time to do more than just get through each day, then maybe I will. But you don't need me to believe, Abby, and you know it. You aren't me. You aren't Tess, even if parts of you remind me of her. You're you. You get to make your own choices. I get to make mine."

"Oh."

"I'd have lied to anyone else if they'd asked me, you know," Claire says. "Lies are a lot easier than the truth. Simpler."

Like Tess, who picked what she knew over stepping into the unknown with Claire for everyone to see.

Like me, because I want Eli but said, "I don't know what to do," because it was easier than saying "I've wanted to kiss you too."

"Do you want—the pictures that Tess has, do you want them?"

"No," Claire says. "I remember them, and that's enough." She nudges me with her foot. "Go home so I can sleep."

"I feel like—I want to fix things for you," I say. "This isn't . . . something should happen for you now. Something good, I mean."

"I'm responsible for me," Claire says. "You be responsible for you."

"That's it?"

Claire smiles at me again, a little sadly this time. "That's it. See you tomorrow, okay?" And then she lets herself inside her house and shuts the door.

I look at it for a moment, and then I walk home.

forty-two

In the morning, my parents tell me I don't have to go to school.

"Why?" I say, because my parents never let me miss school unless I've woken up covered with spots (chicken pox, third grade) or thrown up in front of them (sixth grade). "Is it—did the phone ring when I was in the shower? What's happened to Tess?"

Mom puts down the cup of coffee she's drinking.

"Nothing's happened," she says, and, when she catches my eyes, repeats it again, gently. "Abby, nothing's happened."

"But you never let me miss school."

"After last night," Dad says, "and with Tess being moved so soon, your mother and I thought—we thought you might want to see her. Spend time with her."

"All day?" I wish the thought of spending a whole day with Tess filled me with joy, but it doesn't. I just—not only do I not know who Tess really was anymore, I don't think I can spend an entire day watching her lie there. Watching her live with her eyes wide shut.

"No," Mom says. "Your father and I—we need to see her this afternoon. We need to talk to the doctor, and we also have to start making a list of things we need to get for her new . . . for her new room."

Dad puts his coffee cup down and gets up from the table then, goes and looks out the kitchen window. His shoulders are slumped, defeated-looking. Sad.

"She could still wake up," I say, not because I feel like I have to, but because I still think she could.

I just don't know if she will.

"Yes," my mother says, her voice tight and as sad as the slump of my father's shoulders, but Dad turns around and gives me a small half smile. Not of thanks, but of shared hope.

I smile back.

"Last night, you went out," he says. "Your mother and I assumed—"

"Claire," I say, and he nods. "Is she . . . how is she?"

I look at my parents. What do I say? That Tess really hurt her, broke her in ways even they don't know about? That she saw Tess's need to be who everyone wanted her to be more clearly than me, and I thought I'd seen her true self—the way she was capable of being cruel, the way she could be under-standing without having to say a word—but that I had no idea who Tess really was? That I'm not sure even Tess did?

"She's busy," I say. "Working a lot."

"And what happened with Tess?"

"She said—" I pause, looking closely at my parents, and realize that it's not that they couldn't handle me telling them what Tess did. It's that they don't need to know. They are carrying so much now, paying for a life for Tess that none of us could have ever seen, and then having to watch her live it. Watch her live life still, and silent.

"It was a long time ago," I say. "Claire's—she's got Cole now. She says . . . she says that and work are her life."

Mom looks at me, and I can tell she knows there are things I'm not saying. I can also tell she won't ask what they are. That she understands that sometimes you can't fix things.

"I should go get ready," I say. "To go to the hospital, I mean."

"You want a ride to the ferry?" Dad says, smiling at me. His smile looks so much like Tess's, and I don't know if I'll ever see Tess smile again.

None of us do.

forty-three

I haven't seen Tess in the morning since pretty soon after the accident, when everything was still a crazy blur, and when I get to the hospital, I'm surprised by how things in her ward are exactly the same as they are in the afternoon and at night.

I thought maybe the nurses would be less tired-looking or—I don't know. I guess I thought the morning might be more hopeful somehow. Riding across the river with the sun shining on my face, and thinking about what Claire said about belief, made me wonder if things could be different for me. Better.

And so I thought maybe I'd only been seeing the hospital for what it had carved out of me, what it had put in my heart, all the fears about the future, all my worry for Tess. All my anger at her. And I'd thought that trying to move past that would make it different.

But it doesn't. It's still sad to see all the patients lying motionless, to hear nothing as I walk by their rooms except the sound of machines.

It's how Tess's room sounds. For so long I've been focused on wanting her to wake up, on willing it, that I don't think I've ever—I thought about the machines, about her hooked up to them, but I don't know if I've ever really seen it.

If I've let myself.

I can see why Claire comes here and thinks *No*. I am used to coming in and focusing on Tess.

Or, lately, on Eli.

But now I see that Tess, beautiful Tess with her long, gorgeous hair and still, stunning face, is gone. Maybe not forever—I don't want to believe she's never coming back, I want to believe that one day she'll open her eyes—but right now, she isn't here. Not the Tess I knew. Not the Tess I don't know.

I sit down next to her.

"I—we need to talk," I say, and realize this is the first time since the accident I've said this to her. Before I have said her name, pleading, or gone straight into saying things I thought would bring her back. Make her open her eyes.

But now I just want to talk to her.

"I saw Claire last night," I tell her. "I—there was a lot about you I didn't know, Tess. About you and Claire. You and Beth too. Even you and Mom and Dad. I always . . . you always seemed so perfect to me. So sure of who you were, and so quick to judge anyone who didn't live up to your standards. That's why I thought you stopped talking to Claire, you know. Because she did something you wouldn't, and I thought—I thought you'd decided she wasn't worth your time."

I touch her hand, not because I'm expecting or even hoping for it to move. I touch it because she is my sister. If she was awake, I don't know if she'd let me. I don't even know if she'd still be listening.

There is so much I don't know about her, and I touch her hand because I wish I had the chance to know the real her, even if what I've learned has made me see that Tess wasn't perfect.

Tess is human, just like me.

"I guess you did decide that," I say. "Just not . . . not like how I thought. How could you do it? I can understand why you didn't—I see why you were afraid to come out, sort of. I always thought how people talked about you was annoying because it made me into nothing. But you—did you feel like it made you into nothing too? Like you had to be how people thought you were and not who you are?"

I lean forward, watching her closed eyes. Wondering what I would see if they opened.

"You hurt Claire," I say. "You hurt her a lot, and maybe you were scared, but you—it was cruel. And now, after I find out about you and her, I still don't—how could you do it, Tess? How could you break her heart and then ruin her life? Was it—Claire says it was because you never expected her to find someone else, even if it was for a little while. Is that true?"

There. I see it again, a tiny flutter behind her closed eyes.

ELIZABETH SCOTT

Maybe what the doctor said is true. But maybe what I thought is true too. Maybe, somewhere, somehow, Tess can hear me.

"I want you to be sorry," I say. "I want you—I want you to know that when someone offers you their heart, you shouldn't push it away. I mean, how often are you going to get that? I haven't had to deal with it, but if it ever does happen I know I wouldn't . . ."

I trail off, because I have. Because instead of telling Eli I've wanted to kiss him too, I backed into fear, into saying something easy. Into saying "I don't know what to do," when I did know what I wanted to do.

When I did—and do—know that I want him.

So I tell her about Eli. I tell her what I did. What I want. And then I just sit with her for a while longer, describing how the sunshine spreads across the room, and then how the ferry sounds when it's crossing the river, how the waves break when the boat passes through them.

"They come back though, you know," I tell her before I leave. "The ferry goes through them, but if you look back, you can see them again."

Before, I would have said that Tess should do that. Be like those waves. Come back. Wake up. But now I just say, "Bye, Tess," and go.

I can't make things happen for Tess. I can't make her change the things she did. I can't make her come back.

But I can do something for me. For my life.

forty-four

As I'm leaving the hospital, part of me hopes that I'll run into Claire, or Clement, or . . . someone. Anyone. I really would like to talk to both Claire and Clement—Claire, to see how she is, although if last night made me see anything, it's that Claire is even stronger than I thought she was, and Clement—I'd just like to say hi. See how he is.

Maybe I should wait for my parents. Make sure they're okay. They have to see Tess and do more than just talk to her. They have to arrange for her to be moved out of the hospital. They have to plan the rest of her life for her now. I don't think they ever thought they'd have to do that.

I stand next to my bike, and glance back at the hospital. I

don't see Clement outside. I bet I could find him if I went back in, though. I could find Claire too.

I could keep myself so busy I'd have no time to do anything.

I can make sure I don't see Eli again. It would be easy. It would be so easy.

I get on my bike, though, because the thought of not seeing him again gets to me. Really gets to me. And I think that's okay. I think it might be all right for me to . . . for me to like him.

For me to let him like me.

When I get to Saint Andrew's, the parking lot is filled with boys getting into their expensive cars, and there's an ease about how they move, as if they know the world is okay, full of promise, and always will be.

I only ever saw one person in Ferrisville move that way. Tess. She had such careless grace, made everything look so simple, and it turns out she was more uncertain about herself, about everything, than I thought.

She was capable of carelessness, though. She wrecked her own heart. She wrecked Claire's.

For ages, I've told myself I don't want to be like Tess, but part of me did. Even after Jack, after I swore to myself that wanting another person in my heart and life was over, part of me still wanted to be the girl who everyone knew, who everyone loved.

I don't want to be like Tess now, though. I don't care if I'm a shadow girl in the eyes of everyone in Ferrisville forever.

I just want the people who see me, who really see me, in my life.

I just want to be me.

I feel so brave, thinking that. So proud. Then I see Eli, walking toward the parking lot alone, looking off into the distance like he can't see anything or anyone, and I don't feel quite so brave anymore.

Why would he ever want me? And how can I compete with the shiny-haired, shiny-eyed, soft-voiced girls who live in Milford, who are born knowing what to do in every situation or can at least fake it better than I'll ever be able to?

Because I understand him. I see the way he's walking, how he's really and truly looking off into the distance. Putting himself somewhere that isn't here. He knows what it's like to have people look at you and only see certain things. For me, it's Tess. For him, it's his OCD or his looks.

He is more than how he looks or how his fingers are moving restlessly, counting out a rhythm he has to.

And I am more than Tess.

I walk over to him. I practically have to walk into him before he sees me.

"Oh," he says, looking startled and, I think—I hope—happy, and then he looks off to the side, looks away from me. "I didn't think—what are you doing here?"

"Tess," I say, and hate myself for how easy it is for me to say that. How easy it is for me to not say what I want to. How easy it would be to make this an ending.

I broke my own heart once. I gave it to someone who I knew didn't want it, and had to take it back when he refused to hold it.

I could break my own heart again now. I could just tell Eli

that Tess's going to be moved. Thank him for everything. Tell him I'm sorry she didn't wake up to see him. Never mention the kiss. Never mention anything I want to.

"Is she all right?" he says, looking at me now, and I see hurt in his eyes. I'm not imagining that. I know what hurt looks like. I spent ages with it written all over me.

"She's—she's the same," I say. "But I . . . I actually didn't come here to talk about her."

"You didn't," he says, and it's not a question. His voice is flat, his eyes are still so wary, and I—

I've hurt him.

"I'm sorry," I say. "About the other day. I wanted . . ."

You, is all I have to say. You, just three letters and all true, so true.

"I didn't mean what I said," I say, because "You" is stuck inside me, trapped by fear.

It's just—why now? Why me? I can't answer those questions, and if I don't know, then how can I move forward? I tried to create happiness before, tried to make myself a happily ever after, and it didn't work.

I believed, and look what happened.

"What did you mean?" Eli says, still looking at me, right at me, and that's when I realize that this moment, this now—this is my chance, if I'm willing to take it.

If I can believe again.

And I do. "I meant that when you kissed me, I didn't—"

"Know what to do?" Eli says and turns around, walking back onto the empty school grounds. Walking away from me.

"Wait a minute," I say, and walk after him even though everything in me says to take the familiar path, to just yell something easy, to yell words that mean nothing and just go. But I don't. "Could you at least let me finish what I want to say?"

He stops and turns to face me. "I said I was someone who wants to kiss you. I—I said that and you said you didn't know what to do. That's . . . it's the kind of thing people say before they break your heart."

"But I—"

"It's what Jack said to you, right?" he says before I can say anything else. "It's what my parents said to me before they sent me here. 'We don't know what to do about you, Eli. We just don't know what to do.' And then that was it. I was gone. My life with them—done."

"But I—" I say again, and he shakes his head.

"I . . . why didn't you want to kiss me?" he says.

And now I see what has been there all along, what I've noticed but never truly understood until now.

Eli is as uncertain as I am, as we all are. Life has surprised him like it has me. Has hurt him like it has me.

And for once I know that words will not do. Words will just fill up the space I built between us so easily.

So I don't speak. I just kiss him.

"Oh," he says when I pull away, and then smiles at me, a giddy, glorious smile that turns me inside out. "Why didn't you just say that before?"

"I was trying—" I say, and break off, make myself stop.

Make myself be honest.

"I was afraid. You make me—I'm happy when I'm with you and I . . . I want that. I want you."

He smiles again, a smile that should stop the world but doesn't because it's shining on me, just me, and leans in, touching my face with one hand.

"Abby," he says, and he doesn't have to say he wants me too because I see it. It's written in his eyes, in his smile as our mouths meet again.

I kiss him back and open my arms to him, touching his shoulders, his arms, and his hair. Touching him. I let myself go. I let myself have this moment.

I let myself be here because this is where I want to be.

I let myself open my arms, my heart, because I'm ready to believe in happiness.

I'm ready to believe in me.